Joe Ally; Chemistry Teacher

By
David Carlyle

Purpose Publishing
1503 Main Street #168 ⚥ Grandview, Missouri
www.purposepublishing.com

Copyright © 2018 David Carlyle
ISBN: 978-0-9997999-5-6

Editing by Darci Jordan
Book Cover by PP Team of Designers

Chapter 1

The Plane Crash

Joe Alley, the chemistry teacher at Idalou High School in Texas, boarded a Boeing 747 at London Heathrow Airport, after an unpleasant Christmas visit to his dad. He looked forward to a long sleep on a boring evening flight over the Atlantic. But as he walked down the center aisle to look for a vacant seat, he saw SueAnn Thomas in a window seat, near the left wing of the plane, adjacent to an empty seat. His spirits fell when he saw SueAnn, an English teacher at IHS, because he felt obligated to sit by her, and she would likely talk up a storm. He had to admit, SueAnn looked attractive in her conservative blue dress, matching flip-flops, and chocolate-brown hair. He imagined he cut a fine figure as well, in his new blue slacks, his too tight red T-shirt that showed off some muscle, along with his worn flip-flops. He sat, and she talked. SueAnn had begun to work at IHS in 1959, a year before Joe had started a little over two years ago, but he was only barely acquainted with her. She asked, "How are your twins?"

"Fine."

"How old are they now?"

"Four."

"How'd they take their Mom's death?"

"OK"

"How are you taking it?""OK." Joe realized his last answer was a lie., but he said it anyway. He and his wife had married during their senior years at Texas Tech, and she'd been gone since their twins were not quite two years old. He missed her every single minute of every single day. He did not elaborate, however, and tried to look as if he might fall asleep the moment the plane took off, and indeed, he did.

He remained asleep until SueAnn shook his arm to awaken him. When he awoke, he remained sleepy but noticed a stewardess standing to SueAnn's right, by an emergency escape door. SueAnn pointed out the window. Joe looked and saw what appeared to be old-style tracers shooting past the wing of the airplane. SueAnn trembled, and Joe thought he should try to comfort her. He put his arm over her shoulders and pulled her close. Her touch did not seem as disagreeable as he thought it might, so he pulled her closer. He grinned. "Somebody's trying to scare the bejabbers out of us, but their aim is bad. They're not even getting close." SueAnn continued to tremble, until a bullet hit the wing fuel tank; the tank exploded, and the part of the wing beyond the tank fell off.

Joe too felt afraid then, but the pilot kept the plane upright, although it fell out of the sky and hit the water with a jolt. The stewardess opened the door when the plane hit the water and pointed out. Joe stood and pulled SueAnn up as well, but she screamed that she could not swim. Joe did not release his arm around her as he jumped, or as he crossed his right foot in front of her and used it to push away from the burning wing stub.

He offered an unusual—for him—and rusty prayer, slid his hand down her right arm and grasped her wrist before they hit the water, so if she panicked, he might be able to fight her off, and she wouldn't drown them both. They went down and down under the water before they started back up. When they popped up, with Joe's grasp still on SueAnn's wrist, he pulled her away from the plane, said, "The plane might blow," and swam as fast as his one arm could take him away from it. It blew, but they were away from it before it did.

After what seemed like hours, he saw lights approaching. Joe yelled, but didn't expect a result; however, he felt a hand on his shoulder in the middle of a yell. The lights were attached to a U.S. Navy ship, which had been searching the area under the command of its captain; the captain had put out a small boat, manned by four sailors, who helped Joe and SueAnn onto the main ship. After they safely boarded the ship, the crew continued to search but found no one alive. Some sailors told Joe they were part-way across the Atlantic, and they'd soon rendezvous with another Navy ship, headed to New York.

Joe realized he had not seen SueAnn since they boarded the big ship. When he asked about her, an officer told him she had been half-drowned, but they had been working with her, and they were sure she would be all right. The officer told him she had been lucky—there'd only been two survivors of the crash.

Because ships are slower than airplanes, Joe and SueAnn were a couple of days late getting back to IHS after the Christmas break. But when they called ahead, Principal Ronald Wilson seemed understanding; they had plenty of time to talk on the ship. Joe felt more talkative than he had in London. SueAnn took the initiative again. She told Joe, "I went to see my parents in London. They were there on vacation, and I joined them."

Joe replied, "Yeah I went to see my dad. I'd not been home since I left for Texas Tech; my dad paid for the London trip, so I went."

"Where'd you grow up?"

"In Post, near Lubbock; my dad went to Texas Tech, and he thought it the only school fit to attend."

"Your dad lives only as far away as Post, and you haven't visited?"

"No, we were...estranged for a while, but he invited me to vacation with him in London. He paid for my plane tickets. He will not last long because he drinks like a fish and smokes like a chimney. As soon as he kicks off, I can go to Post, stick 'I am in the ground, and won't have to think about him anymore."

SueAnn slapped his forearm and said, "What a thing to say, Joe. You plan to call him, I guess, to tell him you're OK?"

"I don't think he'd care. Where'd you grow up?" "Joe! Of course, he'd care."

"He wouldn't believe me. Where'd you grow up?"

"In western Missouri, near a small town called Fiskur. And I've already called my parents to tell them I'm all right."

"Why'd you come all the way out to Lubbock to attend college?"

"I can't explain it. My parents just wanted me to get away from home and stand on my own feet I guess."

"You probably only graduated a year ahead of me. Why didn't we have some classes together?"

"I think we did have a speech lecture together and an American History class as well. Remember, in speech class, we had a lecture with hundreds of people in it, then went to labs with only a few. I always sat near the back during the lecture, but I think I saw you up around the middle of the room a couple of times. And likewise, in American History, except we didn't follow that up with labs."

"Yes, I did usually sit around the middle, in both classes." Joe did not understand why, but he felt pleased SueAnn had noticed him.

School began after the Christmas break at IHS on Wednesday, January 2, 1963, but Joe and SueAnn did not show up until Friday in the late afternoon.

Principal Wilson told them to begin work on Monday officially. They ate dinner at several nice restaurants in Lubbock, each evening from Wednesday through Sunday. SueAnn thought of each dinner as a date; Joe might have, as well, but tried to avoid the thought of a date.

Chapter 2

Return to Work

Monday, after school ended for the day at 3:30 pm, Joe sat at his desk in the chemistry room, when SueAnn burst in, trembling, and said, "A huge guy came into my room, stood in front of my desk, and said, 'Keep your nose out of it. And no Police'."

"Keep your nose out of what?"

"I... don't know. But the guy had shoes on as Coach Bolivan wears."

"Did he appear to be Coach Bolivan?"

"I don't know. He had a mask over his face."

Joe went to his classroom door and looked both ways. He said, "I think it's time for you to go home. Do you have your car here?"

"No, since I live only a block and a half from the school, I usually walk. It's a good time to pray, while I walk."

Joe grinned. "You poor girl. It's a wonder you're not worn to a nub." Then he looked soberer. "I'll take you in my truck. I pray...infrequently...too, sometimes, but now, let's go."

They hurried out of the school, jumped in Joe's old pickup and began the short ride. SueAnn gave directions, Joe soon pulled into the driveway of the apartment she shared with Home

Economics teacher, Jan Evans, went around to her side, opened the door, and she stepped out. He went back to his side, entered the truck, and waited until she closed the apartment door behind her. But before he started his engine, he heard a scream, and SueAnn came running back out the door, trembling again. Joe jumped out of the truck and ran to meet her. She said, "I... went in, and saw...a bunch of big rattlesnakes. There might have been...more I didn't see."

"Is Jan home?"

"No. She has a date with Tom tonight." "Do you have your door key?"

She fumbled in her purse a moment, then said, "Yes."

"Let me have it. I will put it in the door lock and call the police about the snakes. In the meantime, you're going home with me."

"No... No."

"You'll be safe. I will sleep on the couch tonight. You can have my room upstairs next to the boys. In any case, you're going home with me this evening."

"Well...maybe."

"Not maybe. You are." Joe took her arm, walked her to the passenger side of his truck again, opened the door, and pushed her in.

They drove to Joe's house in eastern Idalou. Joe again got out, opened the door on SueAnn's side of the pickup, walked her to the door of the house, and opened it. He entered ahead of her; she came through the door, he closed and locked the door, and went up the stairs. She followed. He opened the door to the twins' room. SueAnn looked in, saw them sleeping peace-fully, and loved them, but Joe closed the door. Next, he opened another door, and said, "This'll be your room tonight; there's a bathroom in there, too. Let's go back down for now."

They went back down the stairs. SueAnn recognized Helen, a petite, excellent student from her third hour American Litera-ture class, asleep on the couch. Joe looked at the tops of her eye-lids and grinned. He commented that he saw the tops of more eyelids in chemistry class than he could count. SueAnn grinned too and slapped him on the forearm. "You do not!"

Joe awakened Helen with a gentle touch. SueAnn wanted to demand that Helen explain her presence, and to explain her own presence, but she didn't. She decided she'd explain to Helen in class on Tuesday, and Helen would explain as well. Joe took a few bills out of his billfold, gave them to Helen, and watched her for a moment through a front window. Then he said, "She's home now. She lives next door. I hire her and her mom to watch the twins sometimes." Then he went to the kitchen and telephoned the police about the snakes in the apartment SueAnn shared with Jan Evans Home Economics teacher at IHS.

Joe picked up the TV remote from the top of the TV and handed it to SueAnn. "Pick out something you like to watch. We'll watch for a while before you go upstairs to bed."

SueAnn continued to tremble, surfed the channels, came across a Cowboys replay, decided Joe might enjoy that, and stopped on it. Joe suspected she would eventually stop trembling, but he decided to hold her close until she did. She stopped soon, but Joe held her for many more minutes until she pushed away. They watched the Cowboys game all the way to the end, and Joe said "Almost ten o'clock. We have to work tomorrow, so maybe it's time to hit the hay." SueAnn went upstairs, and Joe did not.

The next morning, early, Joe's boys jerked SueAnn's door open and stormed inside. They acted only barely surprised to see SueAnn there but left no question that the night had ended. She told them she would be downstairs soon, and that they should go downstairs and awaken their father. They left, she arose, locked her door, showered, dressed in her clothes from yesterday, and went downstairs. Joe and the boys had breakfast ready, and the boys were almost finished eating when she arrived.

Joe said, "You boys stay down here with SueAnn. Helen's mom will be here soon, and I'll go upstairs and get ready for school."

Although the boys were four years old, rambunctious and loud, SueAnn continued to love them. She wanted to hug them but feared their reaction. Helen's mom arrived well before Joe came down the steps. SueAnn explained to Helen's mom why she spent the night at Joe's, and Helen's mom seemed to understand, although SueAnn knew she couldn't. Joe eventually came downstairs with just enough time to get to school. They left in a hurry, and Joe drove fast. When they arrived, SueAnn opened her door and left it open as she ran into the school ahead of Joe. Joe shut both doors, locked the cab, and walked fast. He investigated the English room, said, "Everything all right in here?" and waited for SueAnn's reply before he left.

After school, SueAnn ran into Joe's room again, trembling again. She said, "The...man came again. This time...he talked less. His words, 'I said no police.'"

Joe stood at once, took SueAnn in his arms, and spoke. "It's time for you to go home." As before, he drove her to her home, but this time, he asked for her key and checked out her apartment before he allowed her to enter. For good measure, he did not leave until she opened her door and waved him away. He slowly backed out of her driveway and crossed Idalou to his own home.

When he arrived, Helen seemed upset. When he asked about it, she told him a strange man had knocked and told her Joe had said the boys should go with him. Joe practically screamed, "You didn't let them go, did you?" Helen shook her head, and said, "No, but I might have if he'd seemed more normal."

Joe answered, "You did the right thing. I'll never tell anybody to come here and get the boys unless I tell you about it first. What did the guy look like?"

"He was big and odd looking." "How long ago was he here?" "Maybe a half hour or more." "Did he arrive in a car?"

"I don't know. All I know is he was big, and something about him seemed odd."

"Was the guy Coach Bolivan?"

"I don't think so. He wore a mask, so I couldn't be sure."

"If I see the clown that was here, I'll push his nose so far back he'll breathe out the back of his head. I'll watch you all the way home again today, and if you see him again, point, scream, and run for your house."

Joe watched, tried to forget about it, but then took the boys and went next door to Helen Wyatt's house. He asked Mrs. Wyatt, and Junior and Robby, his boys, to sit at the kitchen table. He asked Helen to tell again about the big guy wanting the boys;

she did. Joe said, "Please don't ever let the boys go with anyone unless I've approved it in advance. And for the next couple of days, don't even let them play outside." In response to the boys' outcry, he said, "We'll go up to Uncle Claude's ranch when I get home from school. We'll stay about an hour, and you can run and be as wild and rowdy as you want to be. More than you could ever be in our backyard."

Joe arrived at school almost late again on Wednesday, but ran down the hall to SueAnn's room, looked in and all around, then said, "I'm taking the boys up to my brother's ranch near Abernathy after school. You want to go?"

"Yes! When should I show up?"

"Come down to the chemistry room about twenty minutes after the end of school. We'll stay about an hour."

"I'll definitely be there."

SueAnn arrived in Joe's room about five minutes after the end of school. Joe said, "As soon as I finish with these students, we can go."

They left about two minutes later, went by SueAnn's apartment so she could get clothes for Thursday, picked up the boys, Joe paid Edith Wyatt, Helen's mom, and within fifteen more minutes, they were at Claude's ranch. Claude didn't seem to be around. Joe knocked on the door to no avail. SueAnn asked, "What should we do now?"

Joe replied as he opened the truck door, "We'll let the boys play as we planned. It doesn't matter if Claude's here or not. They can play with or without him." The boys jumped out, whooped and hollered, ran and jumped, and had a wonderful time.

Junior fell on the gravel in the driveway, got a minor scrape on his knee; he cried and limped, until SueAnn said, "Let me kiss it and make it well." Junior limped to SueAnn, pulled up his pant leg, and SueAnn kissed his knee. He ran away and resumed his play.

After they had been at the ranch almost an hour, a rifle shot cracked. The bullet missed everybody but dug a little furrow in the dirt to Junior's right. SueAnn ran, jumped on Junior, and protected him with her body. Joe ran toward the sound but found no one. He came back and saw SueAnn and the boys hiding behind his truck. Joe frowned and made an obvious remark, "I don't like this at all...We need to go back."

They got into the truck, and Joe threw a bit of gravel getting out of the driveway. On the way back, the twins stole whatever part of SueAnn's heart they didn't already own when they both went to sleep with their heads in her lap. When they arrived at Joe's house, Joe carried Junior in, SueAnn carried Robby in, they put them on their bed with covers down, and then covered them. Joe instructed, "You stay in here with the boys. I'll look through the house and will come back." When he returned, he reported, "It looks OK. Let's go downstairs." They went. Although SueAnn didn't tremble and didn't look upset at all, Joe took her in his arms and held her for about ten minutes. She did not resist. They watched a couple of detective shows on 1V before Joe did this, "It's ten o'clock. We should get some shut-eye" thing, and SueAnn went upstairs.

As on the day before, Joe barely got them to school on time, then checked SueAnn's room before he motioned her inside. Joe intended to invite SueAnn to go again, not to Claude's because of the rifle shot, but somewhere.

However, on Thursday, SueAnn charged into his room, trembling again, a few seconds before school ended. She screamed, "Somebody shot through my window, and almost hit Susan. We got out safely, but I'm not going back into that room, ever."

Joe ran down the hall, looked in the English classroom, and saw the broken window. He thought about what to do as he walked slowly back to the now empty (except for SueAnn) chemistry classroom. He had not thought of anything better than to leave immediately when he returned. He grabbed SueAnn by the hand, and they repeated the steps from Wednesday after school, except this time, Joe drove toward Wichita Falls instead of toward Abernathy. A few miles before they came to Ralls, they saw a man outside at a ranch house. Joe pulled in and inquired, "Can my four-year-old boys play here for about an hour?"

The man started to answer no, but then said, "I guess so." So, the boys played for sixty minutes, Joe thanked the man, and they went back to Idalou. The boys fell asleep as they had done earlier, Joe and SueAnn carried them in, and Joe checked the house again. This time Joe felt compelled to hold SueAnn for longer than ten minutes, and again, she didn't resist.

They returned to school a bit earlier on Friday. Joe went to see Principal Wilson. When in Mr. Wilson's office, he described the many problems SueAnn had encountered. Mr. Wilson replied, "The janitor told me about the broken glass, but I had no idea about the other problems. She does not have to go back to the English classroom. There is a vacant room across from my office. Will she feel safer there?"

"The answer is probably yes, but we can ask her." They asked her, and she moved.

Soon after she moved, however, a big guy wearing a mask, came into her room and questioned her morals for staying with Joe. He said he would kill Joe If she stayed another night with him. SueAnn felt sure the man was the same guy she had seen before, because of the mask and because he wore shoes similar to those the earlier man wore. She immediately went to Mr. Wilson with news of the intrusion. He responded, "I'm inclined to agree with the masked man. A lot of people, including me, think it looks terrible for you to spend your nights with Joe. Can you blame us?" SueAnn ran crying from Mr. Wilson's office, turned toward the chemistry room, and then stopped. She realized she didn't want the big guy to kill Joe, and besides, she didn't want her reputation to suffer. She went back to her second-hour class and trembled for the rest of the day. Joe came down at the end of school, looked all around, and asked, "How'd your day go?"

She answered, "Decent enough."

"What's with the shaking?" "I just do that sometimes."

"You want to stay with me tonight?" "No."

Joe wondered if she'd been put off by all his holding of her. "You sure?" SueAnn started to cry. "Y...es, I'm...sure."

Joe had no idea what the problem could be. "Well, I'll at least take you to your apartment and check the inside for bad guys."

"I'm...ready to go now." She continued to cry. "Will you...hold me?"

Joe jumped to her side and reached around her, but tentatively. "Yeah." The very instant she stopped trembling, he drew back. He did not know if her problem involved him, but if it did, he did not want to make it worse. He walked beside her, a couple feet to her right, to his F-150, opened the door for her, drove to her apartment, walked her to her door, and went inside ahead of her.

But just inside the door, he found a big person with a mask. "Hey, get out of here." He landed a punch on the man at mask level. The person ran out the door, almost knocked Sue Ann down, and disappeared behind a house. Joe could have tackled the man, but to do that would have knocked SueAnn from her feet completely, so he didn't. Joe frowned, and again muttered an obvious thought, "This isn't good." He went through the rest of the apartment and found nothing. Before opening the door for SueAnn, he suggested again, "Maybe you want to come home with me?"

SueAnn cried again. "N...o."

"If you're positive you don't, then I'll keep guard out front until Jan gets home."

"She won't be home until late. She has a Home Economics club meeting tonight."

"Then I'll be here late too." He waited until a few minutes after 7:30 when Jan arrived.

Joe went home, apologized to Helen for being late, paid her, and watched her go home. He went upstairs, checked on his boys, called the police and asked them to continue the watch over SueAnn. From the way they talked, he did not think they took the problem seriously, so he worried the rest of the night about SueAnn but could not go to her apartment because he did not want to leave the twins alone. He called her on the telephone early the next morning and felt relief when she claimed to be all right. Joe arrived early at school and sat in her new classroom until she showed up.

When SueAnn saw Joe in her room, she blushed and said, 'Thanks for being here, but I'll probably be OK today." She turned away, and Joe went back to his room.

Before Joe went to the chemistry room, he wandered down to the gym. Coach Bolivan sported a fresh bruise under his left eye. When the coach left the gym, Joe took a quick look in his desk drawer; he found a mask and cape there. At the end of school, Joe went to SueAnn's new classroom again, and everything appeared in order. But he asked again, "You want to go home with me tonight?"

"Absolutely not."

"Then I'll drive you home again."

"Won't be necessary."

"I'll do it anyway, and I'll wait until Jan comes home."

"She plans to be home early this evening."

"Then I won't have to wait as long as last night."

Joe wanted to sleep in the next day, a Saturday, but the twins ran into his room early. He forced a smile. "I don't suppose you boys want breakfast today."

"Well, yeah, we do." Junior looked exasperated.

"I could go over to Mrs. Wyatt's and get some cat food. You want that?"

"Dad! We want a waffle, egg, and orange juice!" Junior continued to look exasperated, but Robbie grinned.

"Maybe Mrs. Wyatt's cat will cook for you."

"Dad, we want you to cook." Junior's exasperated look almost lost to a partial grin.

Robbie's grin widened. "Yeah. Maybe the cat will cook."

"Don't be dumb Robbie-" Junior might have said more, but his wide grin got in the way.

They all went down the stairs, as Joe grinned too, and said, "OK, I'll cook. Will you get the waffle iron out of the cabinet Robby, and you get the eggs out of the refrigerator, Junior? I'll get the orange juice and pour it for you."

Joe poured, and Robbie spoke. "Nobody pours better than you, Dad."

Joe talked again. "It looks like SueAnn made waffle batter. That's something I won't have to do."

"Is SueAnn our mom?" Junior looked hopeful.

"No, but maybe someday."

"OK." Junior continued to look hopeful.

"That'd be super." Robby looked hopeful too. He asked, "Is SueAnn strong and tough like you, Dad?"

"No, of course not. She's soft and sweet like a mom oughta be."

"Yeah!" Robby grinned big.

"Right." Junior grinned big too.

"You boys wanna go see if SueAnn's OK?" They did, so all three of them went out and piled into Joe's old truck. They drove over to SueAnn's apartment and saw her back her blue Chevy out onto the street. "You guys wanna follow her a few blocks to see where she goes?" They did, so they did, but after only about a block, a dark pickup forced SueAnn's car off the road and into a ditch, where it overturned. Joe pulled up halfway close to her car, jumped out, and ran to help SueAnn out of her car, but she came out on her own, seemingly unhurt. Joe asked, "Did you see who did that?"

"No, but it was a dark-colored pickup." "Yeah, I saw that much."

SueAnn looked perplexed. "Did you get a license number?"

"No, the plate had mud on it; it almost looked deliberately mudded. Let's see if your car looks totaled."

"It might be. Everything I saw looked bent or broken."

The two adults ran the short distance to SueAnn's car and looked. Joe grimaced. "Looks awful. Yeah, you're right. Can you afford another car right now?"

"I guess I don't have a choice. But I owe thousands on that one; It is worth nothing as a trade-in. My dad also recommended I do not buy insurance, so I don't have that either."

"I can afford a down payment on a decent car, but not much more."

The twins arrived and invited SueAnn to come home with them. She accepted but planned to go back to her apartment before evening. One of her first actions, when she arrived at Joe's, was to call her parents. They told her to sit tight, and they would be there that night. SueAnn spoke to Joe. "My parents told me to sit tight. But I do not know if that means to stay here, or to go to my apartment."

"I have no clue what they meant, but I'll tell you to sit tight also, and that means here!"

"I'll wait a few minutes and call to see if they need a ride from the airport." She called and got no answer. "I waited too long. They've already left; they'll have to rent a car at the airport."

"Tell me about your parents."

"Their names are Sylvia and John Thomas. They farm near Fiskur, a small town in Missouri. Dad inherited the farm from his dad."

"I suppose we just wait for them. How long do you think it might take?"

"I guess we could look at airline schedules. I don't think there's anything direct from Kansas City to Lubbock, so they'll probably come through Dallas."

"I'll check." After a time on the telephone in the kitchen, Joe returned to the living room. He said, "I think they'll come into Lubbock at ten or eleven, on Braniff airlines. They should arrive here about ten forty-five or eleven forty-five."

They waited all day and into the evening. While they waited, SueAnn told Joe about the masked man in her room and about Mr. Wilson's comments about her honor. When she told Joe what Mr. Wilson had said, he bristled, and resolved to see Mr. Wilson on Monday before school began. Eventually, about eleven fifty, Joe's doorbell rang. Mr. and Mrs. Thomas stood outside.

John looked every bit the farmer, wearing overalls, about 5 feet eleven inches tall, with pale forehead and almost burned lower face and hands. Sylvia looked like an older version of SueAnn-about five feet eight inches tall, still slim, graying brown hair, laugh lines around her eyes, and with even white teeth. Sylvia started talking as soon as Joe opened the door. "We'd have been here a little earlier, but we went to SueAnn's apartment first. A boy named Tom told us we might find SueAnn here."

"You hit the jackpot - she's here! Come right on in, and we'll look for her." SueAnn stood behind Joe and explained everything that had happened from the plane crash on, including why she was at Joe's.

John shook his head. "We'll buy SueAnn a new car tomorrow, then Monday I need to talk like a Dutch uncle to that Wilson guy. I don't suppose he'll be at school on Sunday."

"Not likely. I plan a few choice words for him too."

They all (Joe, SueAnn, her parents, Junior and Robby) went to SueAnn's church on Sunday morning, then John bought a red nineteen sixty Ford Falcon for SueAnn and after much complaining about starvation by the twins, they went to lunch at a restaurant in Lubbock. SueAnn and Sylvia talked a blue streak. Joe and John glanced at them and grinned at each other; Joe enjoyed the time with Junior and Robby, as well as with John, and SueAnn and Sylvia enjoyed their time together. They lingered over lunch, and then returned to Joe's place. John told SueAnn, "I think you're better protected over here than with Jan. Is it all right with you, Joe, if SueAnn stays here until Mr. Mask-e-o is caught or until the end of the school year?"

Joe tried to look casual. "Of course." They talked until bedtime when SueAnn and Sylvia went upstairs to Joe's room, John went up to the guestroom, and Joe stayed downstairs on the couch.

Monday dawned clear, and for Idalou, cold. Joe, SueAnn, and John went to school early, and Sylvia stayed to meet Mrs. Wyatt.

John parked himself in the principal's office before Mr. Wilson arrived. When Mr. Wilson came in, John went to work on him. "My daughter, SueAnn Thomas, told me you cast aspersions on her sexual purity. I think you crossed a line with your

comments, and I do not like it. If it happens again, I have instructed her to quit on the spot. I'll go home now, but you'd better watch your mouth from now on." John stood and stalked out of Mr. Wilson's office.

Joe stalked in. He said, "SueAnn will stay with me until we catch the big guy or until school ends. I do not care whether you like it or not. If I hear you have been accusing her of anything, I will come in here and beat you to a pulp, Ronnie boy. In fact, I'll look for an excuse to come in here and beat you to that pulp. And there's a room across from mine, a social studies room. I want you to get the social studies teacher out and get SueAnn down there. If you come down there, I will see you, and once again, will beat you to that pulp. SueAnn had better not get pregnant because if she does, I will not even try to find out who is responsible. I'll just come to your office and call that my excuse to beat you up. And you might not survive that one."

SueAnn moved again that day, and Joe moved her desk from the other end of the room to the end adjacent to the door. He did not move his own desk, but in each of his classes, he moved a big and tough boy to a spot by the door and asked him to intervene if he saw a problem across the hall. He said, "You don't have to do anything at all; just be a distraction, and I'll show up quickly."

That very day, during Joe's fifth-hour class, Charley Sunder, the boy by the door jumped up and ran out. Joe followed and chased a big masked man out of SueAnn's classroom. The man remained only a short time, not long enough to deliver a message, and SueAnn bore up well.

But when Joe and SueAnn came to Joe's house, Helen ran out to meet them. "The boys played in the backyard. A big man chased them to the house. He almost acted like he did not want to catch them because he slowed on the porch. He could have caught them. Instead, he looked through the window, and... may have...leered...at us. I think he was the same man as before. He seemed strange.

"Was the man Coach Bolivan?"

"I'm not sure because of the mask, but I don't think so. I saw him get in a dark colored pickup and go away. I didn't get a license number because the plate had mud on it."

Joe turned to SueAnn. "I suppose there's nothing we can do about the big guy now, so let us get the boys and go to the Lubbock High football field; we'll let them burn off some energy there." He turned back to Helen. "I'll take the boys someplace to play every day. Don't ever let them in the backyard again. You go on home now, and I'll watch until you're in your house."

Helen ran out and toward her home, but just as she went up on the porch, a rifle shot rang out. The bullet hit a porch post, and Helen ran inside.

Joe used his telephone to call Mrs. Wyatt to confirm that Helen didn't get hit. Then he said to the boys, "I think we should wait a couple of minutes to be sure whoever shot that rifle is gone."

And to SueAnn, "And you wait here. We'll be back in about an hour."

SueAnn stamped her foot! She said, "I won't wait. If you and the boys are in danger, then I'll be too."

"All right, whatever. Everybody ready?"

They all ran outside, and the boys and SueAnn jumped on the passenger side of the truck, while Joe entered the other side. No one shot at them, but Joe's tires squealed as he got up to speed. They went to Lubbock High, and the boys played. While they did, Joe said, "We don't want to fall into a pattern.

We went to my brother's ranch near Abernathy, then to a ranch by Ralls - we don't know the guy there, so we probably shouldn't go back - now to the football field here. Maybe next could be the football field at Dunbar High in Lubbock, followed by Lorenzo High football field, then Frenship football field in Wolfforth, and possibly repeat after that. But the twins will be sitting ducks in my backyard for a while."

After a quiet spell, Joe resumed. "I think I'll hire a remodeler to widen the hall between bedrooms in my house. I'll take a half a foot off your bedroom, a foot off the boys' room, except for the last seven feet at the east end near the bathroom. I will take three feet off the boys' room there and put my bed in the resulting nook. That way, I will be able to get beside it to make it up and to go to the bathroom. The hallway will become my bedroom, and you and the twins can walk through it as you go to your rooms."

SueAnn frowned. "You don't want to give up your bedroom, Joe."

"Yeah, I do. End of subject. And the end of another subject, I don't plan to quit in response to threats, and I hope you won't."

"I won't."

They went back to Joe's place, but this time, SueAnn got all her clothes from her apartment and told Jan she would continue to pay her half of the rent.

Mr. Wilson quit on Monday night. His secretary found a note saying he had gone to Houston, and he did not plan to return. No one bothered SueAnn on Tuesday, but when they arrived at Joe's house, Helen told him the big guy came back and looked at her again.

Joe said, "I'll go with you as you go back home tonight." Helen's house sat on the east side of the street, as did Joe's. So, Joe walked on Helen's right, to shield her from bullets fired from the west. None came.

When they arrived at school on Wednesday, Joe checked for people in SueAnn's room as he always did, but when she entered, she found a note on her desk. It said, 'You're dead.' She screamed, ran into Joe's room, and showed it to him.

Joe looked. He frowned, and began in his now familiar profound voice, "I don't like this...But I'll protect you with my life, the same as if you were Junior or Robby."

SueAnn held Joe this time, and said, "I know. What should we do?"

"I don't know. It would help if we knew the source of the bad stuff. So, as I think about it, that is what we should do-snoop. Let us take this letter to the police after school and ask them to check it for fingerprints. In the meantime, let's try to keep ours off it as much as we can."

After school, before taking the boys to Dunbar, they took the note to the police station. The police said they'd do what they could. They went to pick up the boys, but Mrs. Wyatt met them at the door, not Helen. Mrs. Wyatt said she wanted to show them a note she found taped to the outside of the window. They looked. The note said, 'SueAnn Thomas is dead.'

Joe asked, "When did the note go up?"

"I don't know. I happened to pass by about noon and saw it then, but it could have been there all morning."

"Did you see any people or vehicles?"

"Not out of the ordinary."

"I'll walk you home just like I did Helen yesterday." He did, came back, and spoke to the twins. "We'll go to the Dunbar football field tonight, where you can play. But on the way, we want to stop at the police station, OK?" Joe went out the front door, scraped the note off, held it only by the tape, came back in, they went back out the front door and entered the pickup uneventfully. They went by the police station on the way to Dunbar, and SueAnn took the notes to the police. The boys played for around an hour, although Joe felt on edge the entire time. They went home without incident and watched TV until about ten. Because his remodeler had not finished the hallway, Joe slept on the couch again. But he awakened soon after he went to sleep and saw someone in the living room. He lay still a moment to wake up; then he jumped up and poked a left and a right to the person's nose, who ran out the open front door. Joe closed and relocked the door but did not sleep the rest of the night. He arose early, fixed breakfast, telephoned Mrs. Wyatt to tell her what had happened, telephoned the police to ask them to watch the house, and when SueAnn came down the stairs, proposed they leave early for school. Joe went down to the gym and saw that Coach Bolivan had a bandage over his nose. He went back upstairs and used the telephone in the office to call the police. They told him the fingerprints on the first note did not match any known criminals but did match the prints on the second note. Joe went back to the gym and confronted Coach Bolivan.

"What happened to your face, Bozo?"

Coach Bolivan flushed but didn't respond to the 'Bozo' name.' "I stumbled and fell this morning."

"Do you mind a quick trip to the police station, to let them check your fingerprints?"

"Of course, I mind. Do you think I'm stupid?"

"I hoped." And of course, that's exactly what Joe did think.

"What does that mean?"

Joe turned to go back upstairs, but said over his shoulder, "Maybe I'll explain it someday."

He went into SueAnn's classroom, told her what had happened during the night and that morning, and asked, "What do you think?"

"I think at least two big guys work together, and that one of them is Coach Bolivan."

"I think exactly the same, but how can we prove it?"

"My free period is the fourth hour. Maybe I could go down to the gym, hope Coach Bolivan takes the boys outside, and tie a string to the mask you found in his desk. Then when he next appears, I can pull the string, jerk the mask off, and we'll recognize him."

"I don't like it, SueAnn. What if he comes back and finds you. You'll be trapped at the back of the gym. And how does a string help?"

"A string will be easier to grab and might not even attract his attention until the mask is off. Maybe you could do it. Maybe you could substitute another mask with string already attached."

"That's a little better, but won't you feel vulnerable if you unmask the guy?"

"I can scream, and you and your student will come running."

"I still don't like it...but we gotta catch the person. So... I'll go along with it."

Joe's free period happened to be second hour, the same as Coach Bolivan's. So, he took the material to SueAnn that hour, she made a substitute mask, and he asked a bright student to take the class for about five minutes in the middle of the fifth hour. He ran down, made the switch, and was back in less than five minutes.

The man did not come back that day but did on Thursday, and SueAnn worked the plan perfectly. He did indeed turn out to be Coach Bolivan, as recognized by SueAnn, Joe, and the students in SueAnn's class. Joe held the guy, and SueAnn questioned him.

"Why are you doing this?"

"You truly don't know?"

"No."

"Do you remember who the heroic person was who killed your great-grandfather Billy, and why he did it?"

"No."

"It was my grandfather, Tim Bolivan. And he did it because Billy toadied up to black people. Billy didn't suffer enough, so you're next."

"That's the stupidest thing I ever heard of. Why really are you doing this?"

Joe weighed in. "Wait SueAnn. Does dumbo here have your great grandfather's name, right?"

"He has that right, and some KKK guys did shoot great grandpa Billy, but still. Why's this idiot coach trying to scare me?"

Joe asked, "Do you know anything about the crash of Eastern Air flight 291?"

"Yeah. My buddy and I shot it down. We got everybody else, but unfortunately, you and SueAnn survived." He seemed proud of killing so many people.

"Well, Bozo, we plan to take you to the police station. SueAnn will call her parents and see what they know. I wouldn't give much for your future freedom."

SueAnn called her parents; they said the name of the person who killed Billy was Tim Bolivan, and he was dressed in KKK garb at the time. SueAnn then believed Coach Bolivan's story, and she suggested to the police he might confess if they pressed him.

Chapter 3

The Marriage Proposal, and a Death

SueAnn turned to Joe, and lamented, "We told Principal Wilson I'd stay with you until the end of the school year, or until the bad guy is in jail. The latter is about to happen, but I don't want to leave either you or the boys."

Joe grinned. "Maybe you don't have to."

"What do you mean?"

"You could marry me. That would get you the boys AND me. Will you do that?"

"In a heartbeat."

"Wonderful. How about fifteen minutes from now?" "Perfect."

They went to Joe's home to pick up the boys, then to her church, and were married that evening. It took about a half hour, but everybody—Joe, SueAnn, Robby, and Junior, seemed thrilled. The euphoria lasted only until the next day, Friday, however. SueAnn discovered a note on her desk at the beginning of the day. The note read, 'Your new husband and his two boys are all dead—not today, but soon. Someone close to you will die today, to show how easy it is'.

Joe and SueAnn came home that day, to find the twins distraught. Junior told them "Some guy came in our backyard and shot Mrs. Wyatt through the window."

Joe asked, "Where's Mrs. Wyatt now?"

Junior continued. "She's in the living room, where she got shot. Nobody touched her."

Joe ran into the room, saw Mrs. Wyatt, and determined she was dead. He ran back out and found SueAnn holding the boys in the kitchen. "Get'em out of here. She's gone. Where's Helen?" SueAnn took the boys to the F-150 and told them to hide on the floor in front of the seat.

Junior spoke again, as SueAnn took the boys out the front door. "Helen came here after school and saw her mom. I think she quit working for us."

Joe went out the front door and left it open. He sat on a porch step, looked up at SueAnn, and asked, "What do we do now?"

"Go to the police. Go to Helen. Comfort the boys."

"I'll do the easy one and go to the police. Will you try to do the two hard ones?"

Joe did not wait for an answer, but ran, jumped in his truck, pushed the boys out and headed for the police station. The first question a policeman asked him dealt with what the boys saw. "I don't know what they saw, but I want them out of it. I don't want you to even talk to 'em."

The policeman tapped a pencil on his desk. "We can't NOT talk to them, Mr. Alley. They might be the only witnesses."

"OK, forget that I was ever here then."

"We can't just forget a murder, Mr. Alley."

"What if the dead person is somewhere far removed from my house when you get there?"

"I don't know what you're getting at, Mr. Alley, but it won't work. We have to come, and we have to talk to all witnesses."

"OK, fine. The boys will be gone when you get there." Joe ran out of the police station, jumped in his pickup, and took off for his home.

He did not go into his driveway but parked along the street. He jumped out, did not see SueAnn anywhere, but scooped the boys up in his arms, and said, "We're getting out of here."

Joe threw the boys into his truck and roared away.

A police car with two occupants arrived soon after Joe left. One of the officers approached SueAnn, and asked, "Where's Mr. Alley?"

"I don't know. He left several minutes ago, acting strangely."

"Which way'd he go?"

"Wait a minute Officer. You don't think Joe's the murderer, do you?"

"Who knows?"

"I'll vouch for him. He and I arrived here about ten minutes ago. Mrs. Wyatt was already dead when we got here."

"You'll vouch for him? How do we know you didn't kill the lady?"

Joe returned, alone, in time to hear the officer's last question. He realized that although they had to tell the police, they were an impediment, not a help. He yelled, "You OK, SueAnn?"

"Yes, but barely."

"Have you been able to talk to Helen yet?"

"I tried, but she's hysterical."

An officer approached Joe. "Where're your boys, Mr. Alley?"

"You'd like to know, wouldn't you? They're beyond your reach. How long will it take you to get Mrs. Wyatt out of our house?"

"We'll not move her until we talk to the boys."

Joe looked again at SueAnn, now standing beside him. "Looks like we'll be staying in a motel for a while. You ready to go?"

"Give me a couple of minutes."

Joe had taken the boys to Claude's house and asked him to keep them overnight. So, he thought the boys might be safe that long. He and SueAnn headed for a motel in downtown Lubbock. He explained to her as they went. She asked, "You think they'll be OK with Claude?"

"Yeah, I think so."

"You think they'll be emotionally safe?"

"Better than in a police interrogation room. They said they were playing in the basement and did not see anything though. And I believe them. Mrs. Wyatt didn't get shot through the window. I think someone might have come in through the front door."

"Maybe, but I hate to think of them out there alone."

"We can't go home. The cops'll tail us."

"What if I go to the motel with you, walk back, get my car, and go stay with the boys.

"They can tail your car as well as this pickup. And it'll take you at least five hours to walk back."

"That might be a good thing. They might have forgotten about us by then."

"Not likely."

"Well, we can't just let the boys be out there alone.

"OK, I'll walk back, and try to sneak away. If I make it, I'll bring the boys here."

Joe looked thoughtful after he spoke those words. "Maybe a better idea is to hire a taxi to take us to Claude's place, and then to bring us back. Claude only agreed to keep the boys overnight, anyway."

"Yes, or we could sneak out a back door, walk to a C-store, and call a taxi to meet us there. Or maybe even better, we could change taxis along the way."

"Great idea. You ready? I'll go, wait behind a tree we'll select as we look out the door, and about five minutes later, you follow."

"Yes, I'm ready."

They went to Claude's in taxis as they planned and took the boys back to the motel. Along the way, however, Joe talked again to SueAnn. "Maybe we oughta let the police talk to the boys. They don't know anything, so maybe it won't last long."

"Joe, I'm torn. I hate to think of two little four-year-old boys alone with the police, but I also don't want to defy the police."

Maybe the cops'll go along with it if we tell'em they can talk to the boys, but only if I'm there too."

"Yes, that might work. But I want to be the one with them."

"Why you?"

"I'm their mom. God told me it's my job."

"It's not. I'll go.

"I insist and won't go along with your notion to let the police at them unless I accompany them."

"Well, whatever. You go, then." SueAnn went with the boys, but the police lost interest immediately when they discovered the boys knew nothing.

When SueAnn reunited with Joe, she commented, "I suppose this puts us back to square one."

"Yeah, it does. And we will probably not figure it out before school starts again on Monday. But at least we know what it's about now."

Joe tried to overhear all talk that weekend by people critical of blacks. But he heard nothing. He did have a few black students, however, and Monday, he asked Sarah Jonas, a girl in his first-hour class what she might know. She couldn't tell Joe anything he thought useful, but a boy in his third-hour class told him about a math teacher who gave him an unjustified F and who'd tried to push him around.

Joe went to talk to Bill Able, the math teacher Sam mentioned as soon as he could after school. Bill turned out to be big, and one eye seemed not under his control. He smacked his gum disgustingly. Joe confronted him. "You give an F to Sam Shipman?"

"Sure did." "Why?"

"Can't you guess?"

"He's black. Surely you noticed that?"

"Don't you think you should give grades based on achievement?" "Bill scoffed. "Not to anybody black, no, never."

"Sam said you tried to push him around. That true?" "Might be. But if I did, I got it done. Who cares?"

"You ever shoot anybody?"

"Nobody but blacks and black-lovers."

Joe left the math teacher's room and added Bill's name to an already long list of suspects. He went back to his own room and found a note on his desk. 'Bye, bye, Joe.' He knew Bill Able could not have put the note there because he had not had time. But he did not remove Bill from his suspect list. He knew Bill had company on the list, however.

He had almost forgotten to protect SueAnn during his snooping. He ran over to her room, found her all right, and told her about his day. She cried and trembled; he put his arms around her and held her as he had done before they married. After she stopped trembling, he asked, "You think I should talk to

the new principal about Bill?"

"No, I think we're on our own. You remember the police problem?"

"Yeah, you're probably right Helen come back to school today?"

"Not yet."

Helen did come back the next day, looking terrible. Joe also felt terrible as he asked her what happened, but he prefaced it with a discussion of his desire to bring her Mom's killer to justice. Then he straight-out asked, "You have any idea who could have done it?"

"Yes, I know exactly who did it"

Joe did a small inward Yes, and asked, "Who?"

"I promised the person I wouldn't say."

"You don't have to keep a promise to a murderer."

"Well, I do to this one."

Joe tentatively added someone else to his suspect list, and after school talked again with SueAnn. "You think Roy Wyatt could have killed his wife?"

"That's preposterous, Joe."

"What's preposterous about it?"

"Men don't kill their wives, .. divorce them or browbeat them maybe, but they don't kill them."

Joe would have liked SueAnn's agreement, but he didn't remove Roy Wyatt from his already unbelievably long suspect list Mrs. Wyatt would have unlocked the front door for him, and it was a tenet of law enforcement; when a wife is killed, check out the husband. He spent a couple of evenings surreptitiously watching Roy but saw no strange behavior. On Friday, he approached Roy, and asked, "You killed your wife?"

Roy seemed almost too calm. "Why do you ask?"

"Did somebody give you money to do it?"

Roy's eyes narrowed. "I think you'd better go home now, Mr. Alley."

Joe went, still unsure, but he didn't remove Roy from his suspect list, and he did say to SueAnn that evening, "Be really careful around Roy Wyatt. Don't put yourself or either of the boys in vulnerable positions."

"You still think Roy Wyatt is a murderer?"

"Just be careful, is all I'm saying."

Joe and SueAnn went back to school on Monday. Joe asked Art Smith in his fourth-hour class and Bob Thompson in his sixth-hour class the same question he had asked Sam Shipman the earlier week. Neither told him anything he considered relevant, and he felt almost pleased that he did not need to add anyone to his suspect list. However, after school, he looked up Bill Able's address. He lived on B Street in Lubbock; he used most of his evening to watch Bill and turned up something interesting. Bill went to a meeting in Lubbock and spoke from the floor there. He gave a diatribe about blacks and 'black-lovers.' The MC smiled at him, and cut him off in mid-diatribe, but Joe felt Bill had solidified his position as a suspect.

Tuesday after school, Joe found the man who had been the MC at the meeting Bill had attended the evening before. Joe told the MC some of what had happened to SueAnn, then asked, "Do you think Bill could be involved?"

The man hesitated, almost too long. "Possibly. I don't know—he's an odd duck."

Joe went home and Googled Bill Able. He learned Bill had done recent time for tampering with an airplane.

Chapter 4

Sam Shipman Gets a Note

During Joe's third period class on Wednesday, Sam Shipman approached his desk, holding a sheet of paper. He said, "Mr. Alley, I found this note on my desk." The note read, 'I see you, Sam Shipman. Don't talk to anybody about anything anytime'.

Joe felt perplexed. He'd stayed in his room all during his second-hour break, and no one had come in. He looked at the first and third-hour seating charts. Students all around Sam's assigned seat seemed above reproach. Who could have left the note? He put his hands behind his head and stared at the ceiling. He noticed a ceiling tile above Sam's desk that looked a little out of place. He went back and asked Sam "Were you at your desk when the note appeared? Did you leave your desk for any reason?"

"Only one time, when I sharpened a pencil."

"Did the note show up during the time you were away?"

"Maybe. I'm not sure."

Joe's eyebrow raised. "You're not sure?"

"It might have."

"Did the note show up loose, as you brought it to me, or did it have anything attached?"

"It had a short dowel rod, with feathers at the top like an arrow, stuck on with chewing gum."

"Thanks, Sam." Sam looked at the boy across the aisle and shrugged. The boy shrugged back.

After school, even before he went across the hall to see SueAnn, Joe raised a ceiling tile, to consider whether someone could crawl around up there. He concluded it would be easy. He told everything from the day and the evening before to SueAnn; they agreed Bill Able seemed more of a suspect than before. They both went to the teacher's lounge for coffee. When they returned, they went into SueAnn's room. SueAnn sat at her desk for only a moment, then screamed. She pointed, and when her scream stopped, said, "Look."

Joe looked. He saw a note. 'I'll cut both your arms off, then shoot you.' He swallowed, and said through clenched teeth, "I won't let that happen, SueAnn."

"I think maybe we should give up, quit, and go to a distant state. Maybe whoever's after us won't follow."

"That's dumb, SueAnn. If we run, the bad guys win."

"I don't care who wins. I just want this to end."

"I know you want it to end, but that's the thing. It won't. They'll just follow us."

"How do you know?"

"I know how these guys think. They will."

"I don't want you dead, I don't want the boys' dead, and I don't want to die."

"Then we gotta stick it out here, SueAnn."

"I hope you know."

That evening, after school, Joe took SueAnn to their home. They'd had to go three blocks to find someone, Mrs. Art Stoner, to watch the boys because people who knew Mrs. Wyatt were afraid. Mrs. Stoner's instructions were never to let the boys outside, to keep the back curtain closed, and to keep the front door locked. At first, she did not seem to be in the house when Joe and SueAnn came home from school. Joe knocked several times, then let himself in with his key. He saw Mrs. Stoner at the top of the stair. She said, "The boys are in their room, and I won't let them out. I'm up here because somebody tried to get in the front door this afternoon."

Joe frowned big. "How long ago did that happen?"

"It happened at three thirty-five. I know, because I first thought the person might be you."

Joe looked at his watch and saw four zero five. "Please don't go home yet, but I gotta talk to the boys." He opened the door to their room and saw them cower behind their bed. "Hi, guys."

Robby spoke through tears, "Did somebody shoot Mrs. Stoner?"

Joe answered, "Naw, nobody shot nobody. Everybody is fine. You want to go to Wolfforth and play today?"

Robby's tears dried instantly. "Yeah. When can we go?"

"About a half hour?"

Joe left the boys' room, and said to Mrs. Stoner, "I'll take you home, and you can tell me what happened on the way." He got little out of Mrs. Stoner, except that she'd be back on Thursday because she remained upset. He returned. SueAnn and the boys got in the pickup, and they went to Frenship football field, where the boys ran joyously for an hour. They came back, carried the sleeping boys up the stairs, and went back to the living room, where a masked person held a knife. Joe picked up a poker from the fireplace, lunged at the person and knocked the knife away, but the person escaped.'

SueAnn stood with her hand over her mouth, but after the person went out the door, she reached for the knife. Joe said, "Don't touch it! It probably has fingerprints on it."

"But if we plan to solve this ourselves, what difference do fingerprints make?"

"Oh yeah. Pick it up if you want. It'll have to be out of here before the twins find it tomorrow, anyway."

"Maybe I'll just kick it under the couch." That's what she did.

On Friday, Joe and SueAnn went early to school. Joe checked out SueAnn's room, and entered his own, early, stood on the desk to be occupied by Sam Shipman, raised the ceiling tile, and studied marks in the dust. It appeared the 'arrow guy' as Joe called him, had come from the direction of the hallway. He also saw a fabric impression in the dust. He still had time, so he went to Bill Abie's room; Bill happened to be there, and Joe glanced at his trousers. The fabric there looked consistent with what Joe'd seen in the dust, but he couldn't be sure. So, he waved, said, "Hi Bill," and went back to the chemistry room. As each new class arrived during the day, he asked the big tough person he had stationed by the door to be sure the door was open during the class and to watch the hallway ceiling tile, as well as SueAnn's room.

Nothing happened that day until the sixth hour when the boy by the door motioned for Joe to come to the back of the room. He hurried back, and the boy pointed to a stepladder, and to feet disappearing into the ceiling. Joe climbed the ladder, looked toward his room, and saw nobody. He looked toward SueAnn's and saw a janitor over her desk. Joe waited on the ladder, the janitor looked at him, removed a fluorescent bulb from a box, and replaced a bulb in a fixture above SueAnn's desk.

Joe backed down the ladder and ran to stand in SueAnn's door. No threat or note materialized. The janitor also came down the ladder, folded it, and carried it away. Joe mentally added the janitor to his suspect list, returned to his class, thanked the boy by the door, and apologized to everyone else for his absence from the class.

After school, Joe went to find the janitor. The regular janitor claimed he had been alone all day, and his ladder'd been in the closet where it belonged, all day. The man Joe'd seen couldn't be found. He went to SueAnn's room, told her about the ladder problems, and she wanted to go home. So, they went.

They found Mrs. Stoner upstairs again, not because anything had happened, but because she thought it might.

Joe reacted to SueAnn. "You know, this upstairs thing, scaring the boys, and hiding them in their room, has gotten old after only the second time."

"I don't like the part about scaring the boys, but still, she's only being cautious, and that's good."

"That's bad."

"It's good. Why do not you check the house, take Mrs. Stoner home, and then we can take the boys somewhere to play."

Joe started down the stairs, mumbling, and grumbling. But he found a smallish person, wearing a mask, in the kitchen. He swung a fist at the person but did not connect. The person escaped out the open front door, even though Joe thought he had closed and locked it as they came in. He checked the rest of the house and did not find anyone.

He did, however, find another note. This one read 'It won't be that hard, will it?'

He did not tell either SueAnn or Mrs. Stoner about the note.

Joe spent the entire day Saturday snooping, but felt constrained to remain near his house, to protect SueAnn and the twins. He found big and small footprints outside his house, pretty much all the way around it He found a small piece of blue cloth hanging to a rose bush thorn. And he found a set of tire tracks in his backyard. He almost couldn't wait until Monday to start to look for the sources of those items. Indeed, he looked around the church parking lot on Sunday for tires. The tread on the vehicle that had been in his backyard had an unusual curve on the outside of it He did not find anything like it at church.

Joe bugged SueAnn to be ready for school early on Monday. He looked at every shoe, every tire, and every shirt, dress, and pair of pants for marks consistent with stuff he'd found Saturday. The most promising, although inconclusive, thing he found was a little rip on Bill Abie's blue shirt. He planned to look again after school but felt a bit discouraged by his lack of discovery in the morning. He didn't look after school, however.

During his last hour class, he saw John Corn, the big student he'd stationed by the door, run out Joe followed, and found a big man with a mask in SueAnn's classroom. The man had a note stenciled on his shirt. It read 'Don't run. I'll kill you here or there'. Joe raised a fist to strike the man a mighty blow. The man mostly deflected it and ran away. Joe grinned. "Did you see he can't spell OR?"

SueAnn grinned too. "He can't, or whoever stencils his shirts can't. Maybe it's a clue. I'm going to check every place that does stencils."

Monday evening, SueAnn came to bed late but awakened Joe as she did. "Guess what. Temple Stencil, of University Avenue in Lubbock, can't spell stencil! Their website says Temple Stencle."

Joe mumbled something, rolled over, and SueAnn went to sleep. But the next morning, she told him again. He didn't seem impressed. "Probably a marketing thing. Probably doesn't mean a thing."

"All the same, I plan to check them out after school today."

SueAnn drove her own Ford Falcon to school Tuesday, and after school, drove into Lubbock to check out Temple—whatever. As she talked to people at the business, she didn't detect skill or interest in spelling. She asked the girl at the front desk about the stenciled shirt. The girl remembered it- although not the spelling mistake- but said for customer privacy reasons, she couldn't say who ordered it. SueAnn explained her interest. The girl repeated, "For customer privacy reasons, I can't tell you who ordered that stencil, but I do plan to be gone from my desk for about five." She jumped up and ran through a door behind her. SueAnn checked and found the name Bill Able at the top of a stack of papers. She left and was gone before the front desk girl returned. She went home, triumphantly told Joe, and waited for him to praise her.

Instead, he said, "Maybe that helps confirm him as a bad guy, but it doesn't prove anything except that he's a Temple Stencil customer. Let me tell you what happened here while you were gone. Mrs. Stoner quit."

"No, why?"

"She just said she's afraid to work here. But I found someone else, a Max Rafael, from Slaton."

"Oh, Joe. Do you think the boys will like a man?"

"I like him well enough. And the boys like me. What's wrong with a man?"

"Maybe...nothing."

Joe and SueAnn were almost late to school on Wednesday, because Max was late. He apologized, said he didn't realize how long it takes to drive from Slaton and promised to be earlier on Thursday. On the way to school, SueAnn complained about him. "Joe, he strikes me as more than a bit...creepy."

"He's fine, SueAnn. You're just prejudiced against men."

"Well...maybe."

Joe received the note Wednesday morning. It read, 'Divorce her, or you'll be the first to die'.

Joe talked about the note after school. "Do you remember what it was like to merely be a teacher, and to not have to put up with all these threats?"

"Yes." She smiled and slapped Joe's forearm. "But as long as you're my protector, I can tolerate them."

Joe grinned. "That's good. Because until we know a lot more than we do now, I think they'll keep coming."

They didn't pull into the driveway when they got home, to avoid parking Max's car into it. The boys rushed out to hug Joe and SueAnn but looked a bit rattled. SueAnn went inside with them and asked a few questions. "How do you like Mr. Rafael?" Robby looked away. "He's OK I guess."

"What do you think, Junior?"

"Yeah, all right I guess."

Did anything go wrong?"

Robby looked embarrassed. "He looked at us too much." "Too much?"

"Yeah, like all the time. He went into the bathroom with us, and looked at us there, too."

"You want him gone?"

Both boys perked up, and said almost in unison, "Yeah!"

"Who do you want in his place?"

Robby looked hopeful. "Helen?"

"Oh, Robby, I don't think Helen can do it. She's in school most of the time."

He looked hopeful again. "Mrs. Stoner, then?"

"I'll try. What if she insists on keeping you in your room?

"She'll be better'n Mr. Rafael."

"OK, let's go outside and talk to your dad."

They found him in the backyard, with a frown on his face. SueAnn asked, "Where's Max?"

"He left. But there're a few things I don't understand."

"The boys don't like him."

"They didn't tell me that."

"They told me."

"Why you, and not me?"

"I'm their mom."

"Well, I'm their dad. Doesn't that count for anything?"

"It would, except they think you're not as interested as I am. And I think the same."

Junior said, "It's true, isn't it?"

Joe seemed distracted but answered more to SueAnn than to Junior, "Perhaps. But look at these tire prints. Look at the funny curve here." He pointed. "I looked at Max's tires, and they have the same curve, but only on the front. These prints look like a four-wheel-drive pickup made them, with the curve on all four tires. And look at these small footprints. I could swear the tread is the same as I saw on the janitor's feet at the school. But I might be wrong."

SueAnn shook her head. "I don't know anything about footprints or tire tracks, but the boys say Max acted...strange, and I don't want him back here tomorrow."

"So, who'll we get if we don't get Max?"

"How about Mrs. Stoner?"

Joe laughed. "You guys don't want Mrs. Stoner, do you?"

Robby looked embarrassed again. "Yeah, we do."

"She'll make you stay in your room all day."

Robby answered again. "That's still better than Mr. Rafael looking at us all the time, especially if we can run in our room and don't have to be quiet. And if you take us out to play when you get home from school every day, it's better yet."

SueAnn said, "I want to call Max and fire him tonight. If I tell Mrs. Stoner you and I'll take your recliner to the top of the stairs, and she can sit in it all day, and the boys'll stay in their room, I think she'll come back."

"Why do you want to take that recliner up and down the stairs every day?"

"Maybe we could leave it where it is, and buy another. We could ask the delivery guys to take the new one up."

"And you'll be the one to persuade Mrs. Stoner, and to fire Max?" "If I have to."

"OK, I'll go along with it, but you'll have to. And I'll want to talk to you sometime this evening about those tire prints."

"Fine. So why don't you take the boys out to play, and I'll work with Max and Mrs. Stoner."

Joe did that, SueAnn persuaded Mrs. Stoner to come back, and called Max. She started, "Joe and I are sorry, but we think you shouldn't come back."

"Lemme talk to Joe."

"He's not here right now. He should be here in about...twenty-five minutes."

"Where's he at?"

SueAnn suddenly felt afraid. "I can't tell you that, Mr. Rafael."
"You say he'll be gone for twenty-five?"

"Yes, why don't you stay where you are for twenty minutes, then
come on over if you want to talk to Joe."

"I can talk to you. I'll be over in about fifteen minutes.

"OK."

SueAnn hung up the telephone, ran out to her car, and drove to
Claude's ranch at Abernathy, where Joe had taken the boys. She
told Joe about her telephone call to Max. Joe yelled, "Come on
boys. We're gonna leave now." The boys got in the truck with
Joe, and SueAnn followed him back home.

When they arrived, they saw Max back out of their driveway
and turn east. Joe followed, but SueAnn didn't. Joe returned in
about a half hour; he said Max went right on past Slaton toward
Post. He spoke to SueAnn. "You might have been right about
the guy."

Robby and Junior were awake and excited. Junior said, "Dad
really drove, didn't he Mom! He drove really fast but didn't
catch up to Mr. Rafael. He drove fast to come back here."

Chapter 5

A Car Engine Seizes

The next day, Thursday, Joe and SueAnn went to school as they always did. When they returned, however, they saw Max Rafael's car in their drive, and Max at their door. Joe said, "Stay in the truck." He parked Max in, got out, approached Max, and asked, "What's up?"

Max looked at his watch. "You're early." "Yeah. What of it?"

"I came to ask your boys what they think of the person who replaced me." "My boys won't be talking to you, today or ever."

"I talk to'em, or I kill'em. You choose."

"I want you off my property, pronto."

"I'd go, but you got me parked in."

"You go by any route you choose, but you go."

Max turned, walked slowly to his car, opened the door, and carefully got in. He started the engine, gunned it, and rammed the house. The car ended up with about a third of it inside. Joe ran to Max's side, and yelled, "Back that jalopy outta here, and leave. Now."

Max did, but bumped the front of Joe's pickup, swung around and scraped the corner of the house on his way out. Joe ran, jumped in the pickup, yelled to SueAnn, "Hang on," and chased Max part way to Slaton again, but then Max stopped.

SueAnn asked, "Why'd he stop? Aren't you going to grab him now?"

Joe responded, "Not now. I looked up Max's address in the phone book, and I want to stop at his place a minute. He saw a four-wheel-drive pickup in Rafael's driveway, stopped, looked at the tires, and came back. He told SueAnn, "Just as I thought. The tire treads have the funny curve."

SueAnn asked again. "Why'd he stop?"

"Who knows? Maybe his coolant all leaked out, and his engine froze or something."

They went back to Joe's house, where Joe suggested to SueAnn she take Mrs. Stoner home, then take the boys out to play. He said he wanted to be home if Max came back. SueAnn did, but Max didn't return that day.

SueAnn brought the boys back to the house, asleep. She and Joe carried them up the stairs to their bed. Joe asked, "What did the boys say about all the commotion out front?"

"Nothing. They didn't know anything about it." "Did Mrs. Stoner quit again?"

"No, she didn't hear anything either, except for the initial ramming, and she thought that was ice falling in the refrigerator. And she did not see the hole where Max's car went. So, I didn't tell her."

"Magnificent." Joe smiled at SueAnn.

"I've got to finish and close up the ramming hole tonight, and if I have time, paint the scrape at the corner of the house. I know

Max's pickup's been in our backyard, but I have no clue how it got there. It also occurred to me that I can check the front yard footprints against those in the backyard, to see if he's been back there too." Joe checked, then reported to SueAnn. "I think the prints are probably the same. They're small, front yard and back. The treads look identical to me. And I'm beginning to think Max might have been the fake janitor at the school. You were sure right about him. I don't understand how I could have been so wrong. Did I tell you he said he came to either talk to the boys or to kill them? I think his notion is braggadocio or a red herring, but I can't be sure."

SueAnn's face wrinkled. "Well, I don't want him to do either. Should we sleep downstairs for a few days in case he comes back?"

"Maybe, I don't think he will, but I'd hate to be wrong."

"Exactly. I'll make a double pallet on the floor."

"Fine. I'll get back to that ram patch." SueAnn went up the stairs, and Joe went out

Max didn't show up Thursday night. SueAnn and Joe went to school as normal on Friday, but Joe found another message on his desk, consisting of a picture of Max's car and the words, 'Your boys won't last out the weekend.' After consulting with SueAnn, Joe went to see John Hinkle, the new principal. He showed him the latest message, and said, "I'd like to take my sons to my brother's ranch up by Abernathy for the day, but that'll make me late to school. Is that OK?"

Mr. Hinkle frowned. "Yes, it would be OK, but I'd rather call the police. If someone in the family of one of my teachers is threatened, then that's a police matter."

Joe and Mr. Hinkle argued about Joe's objection to the police, and Joe eventually gave up. He said, "The police are a bigger problem than Max Rafael. If I can use the telephone in your office, I'll call the lady who babysits the boys."

Mr. Hinkle rolled his eyes, but said, "All right."

Joe called Mrs. Stoner, told her about the note, and said, "Please don't, under any circumstances, let the boys outside, or answer the door."

"I didn't plan to do any such thing anyway. Is the threat level higher today?"

"Great. Not that I know of. SueAnn and I'll be home as soon as we can."

They were, but nothing happened. They slept downstairs on the floor again, but again, nothing happened. Joe almost crowed. "I thought old Max was nothing but hot air."

During breakfast, SueAnn asked, "Is that smoke I smell?"

Junior and Robby sniffed, then simultaneously said, "I smell it too!"

They all ran out; someone had put gasoline all along the lower half of the house and ignited it They stood and watched the house burn, until Joe said, "Let's get in your car, SueAnn. If the truck catches fire, it will probably blow up, and we don't want to be close." SueAnn took her car from behind Joe's truck, drove two blocks north, then turned left and stopped behind a house. They started to get out but then heard a major explosion.

They continued their egress from SueAnn's car and walked back to where they could see the remains of their house. Joe said,

"That one's going and almost gone. We need another one." A fire truck went past the fire, slowed, and drove away. Joe suggested a motel in Lubbock until they could find a house. Because Joe's pickup burned too, they went in SueAnn's Falcon.

Joe came back to Idalou later, told Mrs. Stoner and she agreed to take care of the boys in the motel on Monday. Joe and SueAnn took the boys out to play twice on Saturday and Sunday.

Joe found some empty gasoline cans in his former yard, and checked gas stations in the area on Saturday, but didn't find anybody who remembered selling gas in cans. On Sunday, Joe found a furnished house near the school for rent; they planned to move the following weekend, but that house burned too, on Thursday. One of SueAnn's acquaintances, Beth Nichols, offered to rent her a house in Idalou on Friday and said various friends would guard it around the clock. They agreed to move into it and did, the weekend they'd planned to move into the other. Mrs. Stoner almost quit again but said the boys' need and the people guarding the house caused her to stay on the job.

Joe said he'd like to rebuild his original house, but not until all the commotion ended.

SueAnn and Joe went to school on Monday. They checked both their rooms for notes or bad guys but found nothing. During the first hour, Pete Wesson, the big boy Joe'd asked to sit by the door, got up and ran out. Joe followed quickly and saw a small man with a mask in SueAnn's room, grappling with Pete. Joe hurried to help, and in the melee, the mask fell off, to reveal Max.

Joe grinned. "Well Max, you came back one too many times, didn't you- we've got you now."

Max gave Joe an evil look. "You still don't get it, do you? Your boys will die anyway."

"How you are going to do that Max? I plan to keep you tied up in my rented garage, maybe almost forever."

Max blustered, and it appeared a vein in his forehead almost burst. "We got other people, you know."

"Sure, Max. Let's go."

Joe turned to Pete. "Go back to class, tell the people what happened, and tell them to work on the assignment for tomorrow until I get back. I expect to be back in about ten minutes." Pete went.

Joe took Max by the shoulder, went down the stair, and out the door. He took SueAnn's car to his rented house because he hadn't yet replaced his pickup. He tied Max in the garage, with some rope under his arms to hold his feet almost off the floor. He returned to school and to his class, after being gone only eleven minutes.

Joe continued the class, but during the break between classes, went across the hall to talk to SueAnn. She seemed more at ease than he'd seen her in weeks. He told her he'd tied Max, and she approved.

After school, they went back to their rented house. Max had somehow escaped! SueAnn ran inside to check on Mrs. Stoner and the boys and came back out to say they were all OK. Joe said, "Why don't you take Mrs. Stoner home, then let's take the twins to Lorenzo High to play. You stay with them, and I'll go see about insurance on my truck."

They did all that, and Joe went, but when he came back, he thought he saw movement at the outer edge of the football field.

He drove around there but saw no one. He did see tire tracks, got out of SueAnn's car to look at them, and saw the funny curve on the tread again. He didn't tell SueAnn what he'd seen but remained vigilant the rest of their time at Lorenzo High. The boys fell asleep as usual, on the way home, and Joe and SueAnn carried them inside. Their rented house didn't have an upstairs but was a ranch-style house on one level. The boys' room was in the rear, and the master bedroom, with a bath, as the master bedroom in their own house had had, occupied a part of the front of the house. That's where Mrs. Stoner stayed during the day, while she put the boys in their room at the back.

That night, Monday night, SueAnn heard the doorbell ring. She awakened

Joe, who went to see who could be visiting them after midnight. He found one of their 'guards,' with Max Rafael in hand. The 'guard' said Max approached, carrying a gasoline can, and they nabbed him. Joe thanked the 'guard' took Max inside and said he'd take care of the problem. He said, "Pretty dumb, aren't you Max? How many times did you plan to come back?"

Max passed his hand over his mouth, to indicate he wouldn't talk. Joe said, "Fine. I'll tie you in the garage again, but this time I'll hang around to watch." Although Joe's eyelids became a bit heavy before morning, he managed to stay awake and to taunt Max occasionally. SueAnn came out early, and he asked her to bring his breakfast out to the garage, and then they discussed who might watch Max during the day. SueAnn suggested Mr. Stoner, Art. She offered that he's retired, but she thought he might be willing to come and watch during the school hours. She said she'd call and ask if Joe wanted her to do it. He did, she did, and Mr. Stoner agreed.

After the Stoners arrived, Joe and SueAnn went to school. The day went uneventfully, and they came back home. They found Mrs. Stoner hysterical in the front room, but the boys were all right. Joe went into the garage; discovered Max was gone, with Art beaten up. Art said some people in police uniforms came, kicked him a few times, and said they'd take care of Max. Joe called the police immediately. They confirmed Art's story, and Joe berated them for kicking Art. The dispatcher said, "The guy has a smart mouth."

Joe responded, "Nobody's mouth is smart enough to justify beating up the body below it."

"You want us to come back, and kick you around a little?" "What are your plans for Mr. Rafael?"

"He's an arsonist, isn't he? He'll stand trial for that and will go bye-bye for a few years if he's found guilty."

Joe reported details of the telephone call to Art. Art mumbled something about lawsuits and went in to check on his wife. He stood about five inches taller than she did and called her May; Joe had not previously known her first name. Joe told Art he always took the boys out to play after school, but always took Mrs. Stoner-May—home first. Joe asked if Art wanted to ride along. He did and noted he didn't expect to be needed more, so would quit.

Joe and SueAnn went again to school on Tuesday. As on Monday, they found no people or notes. Joe grinned. "Maybe we're wearing'em down,

SueAnn. We got a couple of 'em in jail, and for two days in a row, we haven't found anything here."

"Please don't say optimistic stuff, Joe. Just when we think we've won, one crawls out from under another rock."

Joe's grin weakened, but only a little. "Well, two mornings in a row is the most we've had for a while."

"Doesn't last night count?"

Joe's grin weakened a slight bit more. "Shouldn't we count last night as a victory? Max is in jail, isn't he?"

"You might be right about everything. I hope you are, but I doubt it."

Chapter 6

Sam Shipman Gets Another Note

During Joe's third hour class, Sam Shipman held his hand up. Joe, in the middle of a discussion about stoichiometry, felt impatient and didn't try to hide it in his tone of voice. "Yes?"

"I have another note, Mr. Alley."

Still impatient, Joe responded, "Hang on to it. I'll look at it after a bit." "You might want to see it soon."

"All right, I'll look." Joe strode, grumbling and mumbling, back to Sam's desk. He read the note. I'll kill you tonight, black boy. The hair stood straight out on his neck. SueAnn'd been right. "Can you stay the night with me? Some people guard my house."

"What about my brothers, my sisters, and my parents?" "Bring 'em."

That night, when Joe and SueAnn came back from the boys' play session, they saw Sam, along with two brothers, two sisters, and two parents stand near their front door. SueAnn asked, "Who are these people?" Joe explained about the note and his invitation. SueAnn thought a moment, then responded, "Of course; we must."

Joe and SueAnn carried the boys in, then SueAnn said, "I'll change the sheets in our bedroom, and"... she blankly looked at Sam's parents.

Mrs. Shipman said, "we're Don and Joan."SueAnn continued, "Don and Joan can sleep in there. I'll make pallets on the floor for...Sam and his brothers in the boys' room, and for us in the living room. His sisters can take the spare room. I back Joe's invitation and extend it for as long as you think it needed."

Joan spoke. "We don't want to take over your house. But we also do not want anybody to kill us as we sleep. We might stay more than one night, but we won't stay anything like a hundred, either."

SueAnn grinned. "Joe thinks our enemies are defeated. But I know better. You stay as long as you feel it necessary."

SueAnn and Joan went to the kitchen and cooked up a better supper than Joe could remember. He commented on it, and said, "Maybe you should stay those hundred nights, Mrs. Shipman— but Mr. Shipman probably wouldn't allow it!"

SueAnn looked sharply at Joe, then acknowledged, "Joan's a great cook, isn't she?"

Nothing happened during the night, but one of the 'guards' told Don Shipman the next morning that they had intercepted two people trying to get to the house. Joe felt anger. He said to the 'guard,' "Who were they?"

"I don't know, Mr. Alley, but we stopped 'em."

"Next time, grab 'em, ring the doorbell, and let me decide what to do. OK?"

"Yessir."

Don said he had to go to work, and the children had to go to school, but Mrs. Shipman could stay the day. Joe explained he'd go after Mrs. Stoner, and she'd be responsible for the boys. He said Sam could ride to school with him and SueAnn. When they arrived, Joe did his normal look-around in his room and in SueAnn's room but didn't find anything. During the first hour, however, the big boy, Pete Wesson, stationed by Joe's door, ran out. Joe followed and saw a normal-size man leaning over SueAnn's desk. The man wore a mask over his eyes. Joe swung at the mask and connected with a solid hit. The man grunted, ran out, and Joe chased him, but he got away.

Joe continued, walked by Bill Abie's room, and saw Bill conduct class in there, with no mark on his face. Joe turned, ran to SueAnn's room, asked if she suffered harm, received a no, and ran back into his own room, after a short, but only a short absence. Mr. Hinkle stood at his desk, looked loaded for bear, and asked where he'd been. Pete said, "Mr. Alley was here, and said he'd step out to the restroom a moment, just before you arrived, sir."

Mr. Hinkle's shoulders relaxed. He said, "That's fine then," and he left.

Joe tiptoed to the door, looked both ways, thanked his class for their support, admitted, "I don't normally condone lying, but thank you, Pete," explained what had been happening all along, and explained what had just happened along with Pete's role in it.

A girl near the front raised her hand, and Joe called on her. She said, "Maybe I can offer a clue. I saw a man watch your house with binoculars yesterday.

I'm not sure who the man was, but he might have been Mr. Johns, the art teacher."

Another girl near the middle of the room confirmed that the person was indeed Jake Johns, and a boy on the other side of the room offered a clue implicating Bill Able. Had the second girl not mentioned Jake, Joe would have discounted the clue. Jake had been his neighbor across the alley from him in his old—now burned— house, and Joe thought of him as a good neighbor. A regular-looking, hooked on Texas guy, he always wore a cowboy-type hat, and cowboy boots, with jeans and chaps. Based on what two girls had said, he'd have to rethink his evaluation.

Joe shook his head. "Wow. I should have asked earlier for your help." He decided, however, to not involve his later classes yet; he had more suspects already than he could cope with, and he didn't want to encourage more bad behavior by talking too much about it.

SueAnn reminded Joe they needed to pick up Sam Shipman after school, and Joe reminded SueAnn he planned to try to buy another pickup after school. They did both, as well as to take Mrs. Stoner home and the boys out to play. Sam accompanied them on all their trips, and as before, when they came back home with the sleeping boys, the other Shipman's awaited them. Joe bought an almost new, nineteen sixty-two F-150 with only 15,922 miles on it.

Don spoke to Joe. He said, "I hope this doesn't come as bad news, but we plan to take Sam out of school tomorrow. I've decided to accept a job transfer to West Virginia, and we'll leave tomorrow. That should get us out of harm's way."

SueAnn also talked to Joe. "I hope this works for the Shipman's. If it does, surely it will work for us too."

"It might work for them, SueAnn, because they're merely an avenue to us. But it'll never work for us. People are after us worldwide. Remember the airplane?"

Maybe." SueAnn sounded doubtful. "For sure. Remember the airplane?"

SueAnn didn't answer, and Joe didn't push the subject. He did, however, go out just before dark and look for people watching his house with binoculars. He saw someone-he wore a big white hat; it might have been Jake Johns-in a tree not far away. He considered accosting the person, but didn't, because he couldn't think why it might be illegal to look through binoculars. He tried to think, unsuccessfully, how he could be harmed by that. He resolved to ask SueAnn if she had any ideas. That night, the best she could do was say maybe the watcher wanted to know their routines. Joe resolved to change those and to avoid falling into more.

The next evening, Joe walked a short way down the street and stood for a while; he watched to see if Jake Johns came out of his house. He didn't see anything, but Jake's house remained dark until about an hour after dark. The next morning, Thursday, he said to SueAnn, "Maybe we should go after Mrs. Stoner a few minutes early, and then take a different route to school, in case Jake Johns is on to our routine and wants to do something about it."

SueAnn responded, "I agree. I'll call Mrs. Stoner before breakfast and tell her we'll be early."

At school, Joe did his normal looks, first into SueAnn's and then into his classroom. In his, he found another note, but not as menacing as before. The note read, 'Get your wife, and then wait here after school. I'll talk to you then'.

Joe showed the note to SueAnn before school started, and suggested she avoid his room all day. "Whatever you think, Joe."

After school, no one showed up, so Joe and SueAnn went on home. They waited a few minutes to take the boys out to play and to take Mrs. Stoner home but had no problems.

Friday, Joe again suggested they change their routine, investigated SueAnn's room, found nothing, but on his desk, another note: 'I would have come, but your wife wasn't here.' He showed the new note to SueAnn and again suggested she stay away. But this time, she said, "I think I should go, Joe.

We don't know what the note-writer might do to you if I'm not there." "And we don't know what he or she might do to you if you are."

"I'll be there. I've decided." SueAnn walked into her classroom, and Joe remained in his. He didn't follow SueAnn to her room or argue further. He had no clue who was right, but he had a sense of foreboding all day.

After school, SueAnn joined Joe, and they both stood behind Joe's desk. Again, no one came. Joe said, "I think it's good whoever it is didn't come. Maybe he or she has forgotten about it."

"I don't think those people ever forget, Joe." SueAnn hadn't looked worried before, but she did as they drove home—by a new route. Everything seemed normal at home, as well as at school. But Joe snooped on Saturday while staying close to home to protect SueAnn and the boys. He walked a couple of blocks down the street to a spot he could see Jake Johns' house, as he'd done Thursday evening. He stood until about 10:30 am, and then saw Jake walk past the corner of his house. He continued to stand, until Jake climbed a tree near where Joe lived, and trained binoculars on what Joe thought might be his front door. He stood longer. Jake came back down just before noon and walked to his home.

Joe went home and talked to SueAnn. "I don't know what to make of Jake's behavior, but it doesn't look right."

SueAnn responded, "It sure doesn't. What do you think we should do about it?"

"You have any thoughts?" "Not one."

"Me either. It is not wrong to climb a tree and look through binoculars. We should just tell the people guarding our house, and except for that, forget about it."

"I suppose you're right."

Joe told a 'guard,' then said, "And don't drag this particular person out of the tree and bring him to me if all he's doing is looking at us."

Joe found another note on his desk Monday: 'I saw your wife Friday. If she's back today, I'll talk to you both'. SueAnn came in after school that day, and a man showed up to talk. The man seemed nondescript but wore a mask. Joe thought he saw a hint of a bruise extending below the mask but wasn't positive.

The man talked. "You two hang around with blacks too much. You had some in your home last week. If you know what's good for you, you'll avoid blacks from now on."

Anger boiled up in Joe; he tried without notable success to control it. He didn't want the masked man to hurt SueAnn, so dropped to a defensive crouch, and answered, "Sir, we'll choose our own friends, without asking your permission."

The man with the mask turned, walked to the back of the room, then out the door. As he went, he said, "I hoped you'd be reasonable."

Joe looked at SueAnn. "What do you make of that?" But without waiting for an answer, he ran to the back, into the hall, and looked for the man. When he didn't see him, he went down the hall and looked in Jake John's room, which was empty.

He came back to his own room, and seeing SueAnn still there he asked, "How did he know when you were here—how'd he know when you weren't?"

"I have no idea, Joe."

Joe looked at his watch. "It's exactly four pm. Last night, we left at eight minutes after. We should either go immediately or wait twelve to fifteen minutes."

SueAnn responded, "Let's go now." They went out, jumped in Joe's 'new' truck, and went home by a route they'd never used before.

Before they arrived, they saw Mrs. Stoner walk toward her home. Joe turned around, drove beside her and stopped. SueAnn called, "You want a ride?"

Mrs. Stoner didn't slow. She yelled, "I quit. I'm done. I should've never come back."

SueAnn started to ask another question, but Joe made a U-turn in the street and headed for their rented house. When they arrived, he slid the truck tires to a stop, yanked his pickup door open, and ran through the open front door. He ran toward the boys' room, but when he saw them not in it, his feet slid to a stop, he grinned, and asked, "How are you guys doing?"

Robby looked upset. "Somebody shot at Mrs. Stoner, and she's not here now."

Junior added, "We heard it—the shot—and came right out. But Mrs. Stoner was already gone."

Joe responded intellectually. "Hm."

SueAnn arrived, put her arms around both boys, and asked, "Are you all right?"

Junior answered, "Yeah Mom, we're all right, but Mrs. Stoner's not here." SueAnn said, "We know. We saw her leave. Do you know what happened?" Robby continued to look upset. "A bullet came through the window."

SueAnn's hand went to her mouth. She seemed to try to match Joe's wit. "Oh." She continued. "What should we do, Joe?"

"Do you know anybody else we can get?" "How about Mr. Crane, next door?"

"I thought you didn't like men."

"I'd prefer a woman, but Mr. Crane might be more willing. He' retired, but still might be tougher than a woman

"Yes."

Robby looked impatient now, on top of looking upset. "You gonna take us out to play?"

"Yep."

Both boys shouted, "Yay! Yes, we're ready."

Joe looked at SueAnn. "You ready?"

She ran for the door. "Last one in the truck's a rotten egg." Even though she started first, she had to accept the label!

They had to carry the sleeping boys inside again, then SueAnn called Mr. Crane. He said he'd walk over the next morning. SueAnn grinned and reported to Joe. When Jim Crane arrived, Joe told him why Mrs. Stoner quit, then said, "Don't ever let the boy outside, but know we have 'guards' out there." He and SueAnn introduced the boy to Jim, then went on to school.

When they arrived at school, Joe found another note: 'You talked back to me yesterday, so it's war now'. He showed the note to SueAnn, and asked, "How can war be different from what we've already experienced?"

"It can't. Let's just ignore this last note."

"I agree. Let's do."

Joe walked past Jake John's classroom that Tuesday morning, and saw that Jake had a bruise on his face.

During Joe's fifth hour class, Charley Sunder, the big guy he'd asked to watch across the hall, jumped and ran out of the class. Almost immediately, Joe heard a chorus of screams from across the hall. He didn't need to think the situation through, but ran behind Charley and saw someone pull on SueAnn; he saw two girls and a boy from SueAnn's class, plus Charley, pull on the guy in the opposite direction, but also saw the guy move in his intended way, toward the stair. Joe arrived about the time the person had SueAnn to the top of the stair, on hi way down the stair and out of the building. Joe grabbed SueAnn's arm and pushed the man who fell about halfway down the stair, and hobbled away. SueAnn claimed to be unhurt, so Joe went back to his class. He thanked Oscar for his vigilance, apologized to the class for his brief absence, and explained it. A girl near the back of the class held up her hand, and Joe called on her. She said, "I'm almost positive the man was Mr. Johns. He's about the right size, and was dressed like Mr. Johns was during my fourth-hour class with him."

Joe answered, "You might be right, Cindy. I'll check into it."

Flex Cheney, a boy near the front almost couldn't hold his words back. "I saw a man and a woman poking through the ashes at your old house, but I didn't see their faces."

"When?"

"Yesterday."

Joe looked at Cindy near the back. "Mr. Johns isn't married, is he?"

Cindy smiled in a dreamy way as she answered the question. "No, he most definitely is not."

Joe wondered, "Who could the woman have been? Who could either have been?" No one had an answer.

Seth Green said, "A neighbor of mine, Tim Klein, told me yesterday I should stay away from you and Mrs. Alley. That's not possible, of course, since I have a class with each of you. And even if it was possible, Mr. Klein doesn't tell me who I stay away from."

Joe frowned. He must put a new person on his suspect list. "Thanks, Seth," he insincerely answered.

Joe left his room immediately after school ended, and walked by Jake John's room. It was empty. He walked back to the school office. While he checked his mail, the school secretary, June Arlington, asked, "Did you hear about Mr. Johns?"

"No, what about him?"

"He had an arthritis flare up and might be out for a week or more." "I didn't know he suffered from arthritis."

"No one did. He apparently concealed his pain."

Joe tried to hide a grin. "Yeah, apparently."

Chapter 7

The Ugly Message Hostilities

On Wednesday, February 19, Joe and SueAnn came to school, and Joe looked in both their rooms as was his custom. In each, he found a copy of the same note 'To Old Black Joe and to Dark and Dumb SueAnn.' The copies continued, 'This didn't start out to be your fight, Joe. But you entered it when you married the Dark and Dumb woman. You drug your sons into it that day, too. If you clean yourself up by divorcing D and D, you and your sons'll be OK. Be sure to do it before I kill you'.

SueAnn trembled again, and Joe held her again. She cried. "I don't want ever to be anybody except your wife, Joe. But I also don't want to get you, or the boys hurt. I think we need a divorce, real bad."

Joe scoffed. "Nobody tells me who I can marry, SueAnn. It's our fight now and has been since the airplane went down. I have no plans for a divorce. We have no plans for a divorce."

"I'd agree, Joe, except your safety and the boys' safety is everything to me."

"Your safety and the boys' safety is everything to me, SueAnn. I'll stick, and that's my final word on the subject."

"Please reconsider, Joe."

"Not in a million years."

"Well…I'll stop talking about it then, but I'll still pray about it."

"Thanks, SueAnn."

The day went without further threats, including at home. But the next morning, Joe found another note on his desk. 'To: Offensive Alley. Divorce Atrocious Thomas, or face justice.' Joe showed the note to SueAnn and laughed. "What can this idiot (he pointed to the note as he said, 'this idiot') know about justice?"

SueAnn didn't laugh, but she grinned. "I have no idea, Joe."

Joe found a note the next morning, though, that made him think the note writer could hear his words. 'Justice means you face the consequences of your acts.'

He added to the note in small letters 'Don't say anything here. Let's get out of here before we talk' and showed it to SueAnn.

Nothing more happened at school that day, but Joe felt all day that something could happen any second. And sure enough, when they came home that evening, although the boys remained in their room, Jim Crane was gone! After a short search of the house, SueAnn implored, "We must report this to the police, Joe."

Joe frowned. "I'm afraid you're right, but we also gotta look on our own. You stay here with the boys and make the call. I'll go to Jim's home, and check. If he's not there, I'll confront everybody on my suspect list."

"Be really careful, Joe."

Joe ran out. He remained away a long time, and SueAnn worried. The boys peeked out of their room, and she beckoned them, put her arms around them, and prayed. When Joe returned, over two hours later, Mr. Crane followed! Joe explained to SueAnn, the boys, and to a police officer. "I went down my suspect list, was just past the middle, peeked into Tom Wendt's garage window, and saw Jim, tied to a truck. Tom wasn't even on my suspect list, but I tried the walk door into his garage—locked. So, I broke the glass, reached through, opened the door, took out my pocketknife, and cut the rope holding Jim. Then, we probably could have walked out, but we ran. Jim runs pretty well for an old man!"

Jim didn't respond to Joe but looked at the police officer. "You gonna arrest Tom?"

"Yeah. And I have to apologize to you, Mrs. Alley. I thought sure Joe done it, but Jim Crane agrees—! guess? —with Joe."

"Absolutely. If Joe hadn't a looked for me, I think I'd probably be dead now." SueAnn looked hesitant.

"Will...you be back tomorrow, Mr. Crane?"

"You bet your bottom dollar. And I'll bring my squirrel gun if that's OK with you two. Nobody chases me off from a job."

Joe said as SueAnn nodded, "It's more than OK with us. I hope you shoot a few of 'em."

The police officer looked uncomfortable, but only announced he had to apprehend an offender. He asked Jim, "You know the address of this Wend't guy?"

"No, but to get there, just go over a street" (he pointed east), "then north about three houses. It's a brick ranch on the east side of the street. Wend't has a mailbox with his name on it, and glass is broken in the garage walk door." The officer went out the front door.

Joe explained about the 'guards' to Jim, then warned: "Don't shoot one of those guys!"

Jim grinned as he headed for home and looked back over his shoulder. "If they don't try to break in, I won't shoot 'em."

Joe looked at his sons. "You guys think I forgot about you? Let's go." Robby said, "Yay!"

Junior merely grinned and headed for the 'new' truck.

They all went to the Dunbar High football field, including SueAnn. The boys had a great time for about forty minutes, but then everybody heard a rifle shot and SueAnn fell to the turf. Joe and the boys ran to her, saw blood everywhere, and saw SueAnn hold her arm. Joe glanced quickly around, saw nobody, and looked more carefully at SueAnn's arm. He said, "It appears the shooter only hit your arm, but from all the spurting, it also appears he hit an artery. Let me tie a rope around your arm; then we need to get to a doctor. Chapman Clinic is nearby. We'll go there."

Dr. Chapman commented, "It's good you had the rope, and it's also good you got here when you did. But your wife will be OK." Joe felt relieved, and both boys grinned.

They returned home, and the boys stayed awake this time. After a quiet spell, Junior spoke to Joe. "Do you think we should stay home in the evenings, so Mom doesn't get shot again?"

"Of course not, Junior. Mom might stay home until she's all well, but we'll go anyway I don't expect anything that happened this evening to ever happen again." And Joe planned to be super alert.

Joe checked the house as he always did, but found no one. SueAnn stayed home the following day, Thursday, February 20, but Joe went to school. He looked into SueAnn's room out of habit, then ran to his own desk; he found a note: 'To Dumbo Joe: I'll fire more than a warning shot next time.' Joe sat heavily in his chair. He ran his fingers through his hair, and tried, without success, to think.

When Joe's first-hour people arrived, he told Pete Wesson, his 'in-the-corner' person, what had happened and asked his advice. Pete stared out the door a moment, then looked Joe in the eye and drawled, "You can't give in to stuff like that. You gotta find the guy."

Joe mumbled "Thank you," and considered the advice. If only he had to find A guy, but he had several that he knew about, plus how many more?

The only conclusion he came to was that he couldn't tell SueAnn about the latest note. He feared his teaching almost fell apart that day, but the day ended, and he went home. When he arrived, however, he found another note on his door: 'To Hateful Joe: Sordid Sue is no more.'

Joe tore the note from his door, showed it to SueAnn, found a magic marker, wrote on the bottom of the page, 'TO WHO-EVER PUT UP THIS NOTE—YOU ARE NO MORE' showed the addition to SueAnn, and started for the door.

SueAnn murmured, "Joe, you can't put up a response like that."

"And why can't I?"

"It's...not...Christian."

"I don't feel very Christian. So I'm gonna put it up." "It... will... invite retaliation."

"So, if anybody wants to retaliate, let 'em." "Please, Joe."

"Please what?"

Joe started again toward the door, stuck the sign back in about the original place, and slammed the door. Jim Crane left and closed the door more quietly. Joe took the boys, and they also left for their play, but when they returned, the sign had been taken away.

Joe made two trips to carry the boys to their room, then confronted SueAnn. "Where's the sign?"

"What sign?"

"Don't act all innocent. Where's the sign?"

"I didn't take the sign, Joe. Maybe one of the 'guards' took it." "If that happened, I'll fire the posse of 'em."

"You can't fire them, Joe. They don't work for you." "They won't work for anybody after I get done with 'em."

"Please leave them alone, Joe. They work for Beth, my friend who owns the house. And they provide a wonderful service to us. I feel much safer, both for me and for the boys, because they're there." She flashed her most alluring smile at Joe.

He smiled back, forgot about the next words he intended to say, and eagerly uttered, "Yes?"

She smiled more, and questioned, "We haven't seen or heard from Bill Able, lately have we?"

"Uh...No."

"How do you think it would work if I baked some cookies, took them to his room and gave them to him. Do you think that would lure him back into the fray?"

"Maybe. Are you sure you want him back into it?"

SueAnn almost ignored Joe's last comment, and certainly his last question. "I think I'll bake the cookies tomorrow, and you can take them to Bill on Monday."

"OK, I'll take 'em if you're dead set on it."

The doctor had told SueAnn specifically not to go to church on Sunday or to school on Monday. So, Joe and the boys didn't go to church on Sunday, but Joe went to school on Monday and entered Bill Abie's room first thing. "SueAnn baked these for you."

He quickly turned to leave, but Bill yelled after him, "That stupid woman?" threw the cookies out into the hall, and yelled again, "She'll get a visit from me tomorrow."

Bill had never frightened Joe before, but his last comment caused Joe to realize he knew SueAnn wouldn't be at the school that day. Could it be because Bill had fired the shot? Or could Bill somehow hear them as they talked? Joe resolved to wait after school until he saw Bill go home, then get the mask out of his desk. Maybe that would stop him. In any case, he also planned to get SueAnn out of the house, where he would warn her not to say much inside.

Tuesday, before school, a huge man showed up in SueAnn's room, with a mask, but not identical to the one Joe had stolen. SueAnn smiled and asked, "Did you enjoy the cookies? Then she screamed and bolted for Joe's room. The huge guy ran out also, and down the hall north. Joe came out of his room with a question in his eyes, and asked, "What is it. Are you all right?"

SueAnn stomped her foot and yelled, "Of course. Catch him." She pointed north. After a moment of hesitation, Joe ran, but the man turned into Bill's classroom, and when Joe arrived, the room appeared empty. Joe saw an open window, ran to it, saw a ladder there, with a big man just stepping off the bottom rung. He smiled and thought: the guy is afraid of me and went back to tell SueAnn what happened.

SueAnn, still mad, exclaimed, "That was Bill! I know it was!"

Joe tried to take her in his arms, but she pulled away. He said, "The man'll be back. You know he will."

His voice dropped to a whisper, "Indeed, we should get home early after school today. He might wait for us there."

At exactly four pm, the allowed time they could leave school, Joe and SueAnn left. As they neared home, they saw two 'guards' hold a struggling Bill Able, plus Jim Crane carry his 'squirrel rifle,' along with a revolver. One of the 'guards' stated they saw the big man at the door, with a pistol in his hand. They grabbed him and asked Jim, who came out to see what the excitement was about, to carry the pistol.

Joe countermanded his earlier instruction, jerked his head to the east, and said, "Take 'em to the police station." Then he turned to SueAnn, smiled, and added, "You were absolutely right, dear."

SueAnn smiled back and acknowledged Joe's comment, then suggested, "Let's do a 'charm offensive,' and hope for loose lips."

Joe said, "I might agree if I could guess what you mean."

"I'm not sure. Maybe we could put an ad in the Avalanche-Journal, saying you'll fight anyone in a dark alley on Mondays and Tuesdays."

Joe smiled during the sarcastic part of his response but looked more serious during the remainder.

"Fighting people in dark alleys will show plenty of charm, SueAnn, but individuals probably exist that I can't handle, not to mention groups."

SueAnn didn't give up. "Maybe we could form a 'strong back-cooking aid team.'

"Yes?"

"Perhaps we can put an ad in the paper to read, Get help for your project. Find at least one more person to help, schedule it with Joe Alley, and he'll bring his strong back. SueAnn Alley will work in the kitchen to help feed your crew. Joe's specialties are building buildings, wrecking buildings, digging, yard work, and ranch work."

"That's half-way good, SueAnn, but what if somebody from Chicago calls. How will that help us?"

"Perhaps it will be better if I make copies to put into teacher's mailboxes at IHS, and limit our offer to teachers there?"

"I can go with that."

SueAnn made an original, ran off the copies, and put them in the IHS mailboxes on Wednesday.

Jan Evans, home economics teacher and SueAnn's former room-mate, scheduled Joe and SueAnn for the following Saturday. She claimed, "Bob Randle, the apartment owner wants to paint the apartment. I've also found three other people, to help paint, and one to help in the kitchen."

Joe and SueAnn showed up and found Bob already there, along with Ed Argus, Social Studies teacher. Bob said Don Arlington, husband of secretary June Arlington at IHS, and a man named Ray Feinberg would arrive any minute, as they did.

Ray seemed to want to talk privately to Joe from the instant he arrived, and after about an hour, Joe and Ray found themselves alone in the same room. Ray nodded to Joe, and commented in a low voice, "Joe, I think you should be careful around Tim Klein. Tim lives next door to me, and a few days ago, he claimed he plans to kill you and your boys." Joe didn't tell Ray he'd already been warned about Tim, by Seth Green.

"I don't think he can do it Ray, but thanks. I'll be sure to watch Tim from now on."

That evening, Joe passed on Ray's comment to SueAnn. She said, "I overheard something useful too. Don Arlington, in talking to Jan, reported an odd thing. He claimed Jake Johns called June Friday and said he'd be back Monday but had to skip out during his free period to 'Knock off somebody.' Don thought that odd, but I think you need to be especially careful during Jake's free period, which is the fifth hour."

Before Joe went to school on Monday, he asked Jim Crane to watch for Jake Johns and to be sure to keep him away from Junior and Robby. At school, he talked to Charley Sunder, the fifth-hour big boy by his door, "I once asked you to watch for problems across the hall and said you didn't have to do anything except be a distraction. But today, if anybody comes in here, tackle the guy, will you?"

Charley tried to work on his homework for the day, and to look tough. He threatened, "I got it, Mr. Alley."

When nothing happened during the fifth hour, Joe shot across the hall to SueAnn's room the instant school ended. "What if we sneak out early tonight?" He explained why.

SueAnn acknowledged, "I understand, Joe. I agree. I'm ready now if you want to go now."

"Let's do." They started out the door but met Mr. Hinkle in the doorway. Hinkle's eyebrows went up.

"You folks going someplace?"

"No Sir," SueAnn murmured.

"I've been watching you two. You left early seven times in February alone. That will stop."

Joe looked at his watch. "After today, Sir, but please let us go today, now." Mr. Hinkle's face reddened. "Why would I do that?"

"Just let us go quickly, and I'll explain the whole deal to you on Tuesday. OK?" Joe grabbed SueAnn's arm, pushed Mr. Hinkle aside, dragged SueAnn with him, went down the steps, and out the door.

"Was that smart, Joe?"

"In my book, yes. We could lose our job, but we could also lose our boys. The job's second to them."

"I agree. Let's jump in the truck and go." They did, but things seemed normal at home. Joe, however, did speak to Jim Crane. "Old Man Hinkle has gotten picky. He doesn't want us to leave the school until four pm. So, we won't be early after this if we have a job at all. On top of that, Jake Johns' free period is the fifth hour, or twelve thirty-five to one thirty, and I think he might show up here someday, between about 12:30 and 1:30, and try to kill Junior and Robby. So, be especially vigilant then, OK?"

Joe and SueAnn made it a point to arrive before 7:30, that is, early, at school on Tuesday. Joe told June he'd like to talk with Mr. Hinkle and was admitted to Mr. Hinkle's office almost immediately. Joe explained to Mr. Hinkle about all the problems they'd had and asked for another chance. Mr. Hinkle looked out his window for a time, looked back at Joe, and inquired, "Did your boys need you last night?"

"No, Sir."

"Have they ever needed you home early?" "Uh...No."

"I won't fire your wife...or you, Joe. But be sure you both give us your entire workday, every day, starting today."

"Yes, Sir." Joe remained in Mr. Hinkle's office another moment until Mr. Hinkle told him the discussion had ended.

Joe went to SueAnn's room. "He didn't fire either one of us, but I think he might if we leave early again." He waited until the beginning of the fifth hour and spoke to Charlie Sunder again, with the same message as the day before. Near the end of the fifth period, a pistol appeared beside the classroom door, and it fired but didn't hit anyone. Charley jumped out the door, then looked down the stair. Joe ran to also look but didn't see anybody.

Charley tried to explain, "I was overly engrossed in the lesson, I guess."

"Don't worry about it, Charley. You caused the guy to shoot without looking, and he missed us all. That means you did good!"

Joe caught SueAnn's eye, and he resumed his class. They left that evening after four pm. SueAnn looked thoughtful, then commented, "We might be down to only two people after us now, and I have a plan to get us down to one."

"Even if you're right about the two-part—and I'm guessing you're probably not—how do you plan to change two into one?"

"Why aren't I right about two?"

"What about the man and woman Flex Cheney told me about in my fifth-hour class, poking around in the ashes at our old house? And do we know who shot Mrs. Wyatt? What about Tim Klein? What if there're a couple of dozen others out there?"

"All right, maybe the man and woman, and possibly Tim Klein. But the couple dozen others are as likely not to exist as to exist. And we'll probably never know who shot Mrs. Wyatt. It was terrible, of course, but probably an isolated incident."

"What if, instead of a couple dozen out there, there're three, or two, or one?"

"Have you considered zero, Joe?"

"I'd like to be that lucky. In any case, what's your plan to cut the number by one?"

"The all-school art show is coming up on March fourteen, fifteen, and sixteen. I think you could do something like you did with the cookies for Bill Able, but with Jake Johns, entice him to my room and catch him· there."

"How is the art show involved?"

"You could go, ask permission for one of my students who's not one of his, to enter a project."

"Hardly any of my students take art. Maybe someone else will be better...or maybe, better yet, one of my students, but you be the permission asker...and don't say the student is mine—let him think the student is yours—still better, maybe you could do the art yourself. You're probably better at it."

Joe also asked Helen Wyatt to stop by his room for a few minutes on Tuesday. He was pretty sure her mom's killer was Roy Wyatt, but because SueAnn thought that idea 'ridiculous' or 'preposterous' or something like that, he didn't mention anything about it to SueAnn. But Helen didn't show up until after school that day, so SueAnn learned that Helen talked with Joe anyway. Joe knew Helen had clammed up once before, so he began obliquely. "How's your dad?"

"He's about as well as I expect him to be. He misses Mom." "Is your dad a hunter?"

"No, that's part of the problem. He just sits and thinks about Mom."

Because he couldn't think of any other question to ask, Joe took a chance. "What did he do with his gun?"

Helen didn't seem to notice the oddity of the question but merely answered it. "He doesn't have one."

Joe took another chance. "I mean the gun he had until last year." Helen shot a strange look at Joe. "He's never had a gun."

"Is that true for you and your mom as well?"

Helen gave another strange look, but said, "Ye...s."

Joe decided Helen either lied to him or possibly her dad could be innocent. So, he branched out a bit. "Do you have any cousins?"

She almost swelled with pride but didn't yell. Instead, she murmured, "Twenty-three."

Joe felt compelled to recheck that big number. "Twenty-three cousins?" Helen nodded.

"How many of them are on your father's side?"

She looked out the window for a long moment. "Twelve." "How many of your dad's brothers and sisters live nearby?"

"None. He has three brothers and two sisters. One lives in—

"No need to tell me all the details. You have eleven cousins on your mom's side?"

She nodded again.

"How many brothers and sisters does your mom have—did your mom have?"

Joe noted that Helen stiffened slightly, but perhaps it could be a natural reaction to the fact her mom was gone. "She had a brother and two sisters."

"Tell me about the sisters. Do they live around here?"

Helen seemed to relax a bit. "Aunt Rose lives in Houston. Aunt Jewell lives in San Antone."

"What about her brother? What's his name?"

She suddenly had a definitely nervous look. "Ralph." "Does he live in the vicinity?"

Helen began to cry and ran from the room. Joe immediately began to suspect Helen's Uncle Ralph but didn't know where he lived or his last name.

SueAnn came into the room with a worried look on her face. "What was that all about?"

"Not much. We talked about her mom is all."

SueAnn's concerned look continued. "I wonder why she didn't talk to me?"

Joe didn't answer. That night, however, he talked again to Roy Wyatt. "Helen tells me you're pretty broken up about your wife's death."

"Wouldn't you be, if it was your wife?"

"For sure. What was your wife's maiden name?" "I'll tell you again, Mr. Alley, it's time for you to go."

Joe felt he'd gotten close, but he left, as Mr. Wyatt instructed.

He next asked Jim Crane after school on Wednesday. "You know what Mrs. Wyatt's maiden name was?"

Crane thought a moment. "No, I don't, but why don't you ask Ralph Johnson, her brother?"

Joe allowed himself another internal 'Yes!' "You wouldn't know his address, would you?"

"No. Someplace in Ransom Canyon I think."

"Thanks, Jim. I appreciate you being here today." He opened the front door for Jim.

He couldn't wait for Jim to go, so he could look at the phone book and find an address for Ralph Johnson. The address turned out to be 102 Hwy 400, in Ransom Canyon. All through the boys' play time, he could think about nothing but Ralph Johnson. As they drove home, he told SueAnn, "When we get the boys home, I think I'll be away for a few minutes."

"Where are you going?"

"Nowhere. Out for a drive."

SueAnn knew Joe seldom went anyplace without a destination in mind, but let it go.

"OK, but I have an art project for Mr. Johns when you're ready."

Joe was torn. He wanted to nail Jake, but also to learn more about Ralph.

He eventually said, "Can I look at it after supper? I don't have a student to take it to him yet, but I can probably find one tomorrow. We need to take the boys out to play now, however."

"Yes, Joe. Whatever."

SueAnn and Joe carried the sleeping twins into the house when they returned. Joe went back to his truck and traveled east. He found 102 Hwy 400 on his first trip through Ransom Canyon but found an empty lot there. Any other time, he'd have gone across the street and asked a few questions but felt hurried, so didn't. He thought about ways to protect SueAnn from Jake Johns as he drove home.

After supper that evening, he acted impatiently. "Where's the art project?"

SueAnn showed him an excellent still life. He exclaimed over it and promised to find a student on Thursday. He added, "After

I find a student to claim it, you take it to Johns after school. To be safe, don't enter the room, but stand beside the door, just outside. And don't forget, it's by an unnamed student, and you'll only claim to ask if Jake'll put it in the art show. I'll stand beside the door too, on the other side. If you can hand the picture to him, and if he doesn't see me, that will be great. But if he sees me, that's OK too. Don't frame the picture, so it will be like all the others."

Joe found a willing student and SueAnn went, according to plan, to the art room after class on Thursday. Mr. Johns didn't see her at first, so she knocked on his door, "Here's a picture made by someone, not your student. Will you include it in the art show?" He looked, then glared when he saw who she was. He reached through the door, took the picture, tore it in half, and threw the pieces back out into the hall. He didn't see Joe, and SueAnn backed away some, along the hall wall. Mr. Johns didn't answer SueAnn's question or say anything at all but stomped back to his desk. Joe made circular motions near his ear with his finger, to indicate he thought Jake crazy. SueAnn grinned and nodded. They each went back to their room. Joe looked back before he entered his room, but didn't see anyone.

During the fifth hour on Friday, Joe told Charlie Sunder about Thursday's events and asked him to watch especially close. About half-way through the hour, Charlie motioned Joe to go to him. Charlie told him somebody came down the hall toward them. Joe looked, saw someone with a mask about fifteen feet from SueAnn's door. He stepped out, as if to block the hall. The man stopped, turned and went back the way he'd come. Joe grinned at Charlie, gave him a high five, and asked him to keep watching. Nothing happened during the remainder of the fifth hour, and when school ended, Joe went to stand in SueAnn's room.

Nothing had happened by four, so they went home. Everything seemed fine at home too, but Joe didn't want to leave SueAnn, and the boys unprotected on Saturday or Sunday, so he stayed home both days, except to attend church with SueAnn and the boys on Sunday.

Saturday, Joe stood in a spot where he could see his 'old' house lot, and the 'new,' for a while. He decided he'd run to the 'old' if he saw anybody there, but he didn't, so he went back to the 'new' house.

Chapter 8

SueAnn Plans a Birthday Party and Gets a New Note

During the noon meal, SueAnn observed that the boys fifth birthday would happen on April eighteen, a Thursday. She asked Joe, "What do you think about having their party on Saturday, the twentieth?"

Although both boys smiled in anticipation, Joe didn't look interested but shrugged. "Have it any day you want, or don't have it. We haven't had one for two years, and another year won't matter."

SueAnn grinned conspiratorially at the boys. "A fifth birthday can happen to them only one time. We'll have a party. Robby looked at Junior, and said in a voice he thought only moderately loud, "Yay."

"I've already invited my parents, although they might not be able to come—April's corn planting time—but I hope. I'll invite Helen and her dad,

Mr. and Mrs. Stoner, your brother Claude, Jim Cline, and the Shepherds—I'm sure they can't come, but I want to invite them anyway, and Terry and Susan Oliver, the boy and girl up the street, plus anybody else Robby and Junior suggests. And you'll invite your dad of course. I'll make two birthday cakes, about a hundred gallons of punch, and a couple of thousand cookies!"

"Wait, go back a step. I won't invite my dad under any circumstances." "Oh, Joe, you must."

"My mom went downhill for two years. He didn't tell me. He didn't even tell me about her funeral. Nope, I'm not going to invite a scummy scoundrel like that."

"Joe! He was awful, terrible, wrong. How do you plan to react?"

"I don't plan to react. I went to London, but he didn't mention Mom. He can sit down there in Post now and rot for all I care."

SueAnn spoke slowly and enunciated with care. "So, your...plan is to counteract one wrong...with another?"

The muscles in Joe's jaw stood out. "Call it anything you want. I wouldn't invite him to a dog hanging, a birthday party, or anything else."

Robby started to cry. Junior did not, but his chin quivered, and his eyes looked like the headwaters of the Brazos.

SueAnn put her hand on Joe's arm. "Perhaps it could help if you take the first step, Joe."

"Why would I want to do that?"

"For Robby and Junior? They need to know their grandfather." SueAnn apparently turned a page in her mind. "I'll write the invitation, but you must do three things."

The conversation seemed to end there, but after a long, long pause, Joe muttered, "What three?" Robby didn't stop crying, but the tear flow reduced, and he almost stopped—not, but he began a series of inhaled gasps. Junior appeared unchanged.

"First, give me your dad's address and next sign your name at the bottom of the invitation, and last, be nice to him when he's here."

"You think he'll come? He won't."

"He won't—On the off chance he does, you must promise to be nice to him. What's his address? I'll write to him now."

Joe told SueAnn an address. She might have been ready already, because the first drawer she opened had the invitation stationery in it, along with stamps. She wrote an invitation and took it to the mailbox immediately. When she came back in, she hugged Joe. "You're a good man, a good father, a good son, and above all, a good husband, Joe."

Joe grinned, and invited, "Who wants to go early to Lorenzo to play outside?" all four of them went, stayed about ten minutes more than an hour, and the boys remained awake and excited about a birthday party all the way home.

During the fifth hour on Monday, Joe failed to look at Charlie for a while, as he became engrossed in his teaching. Charlie eventually stood and waved his arms like semaphores. Joe startled, and ran toward the back of the room, just in time to see a masked person come down the hall and enter SueAnn's classroom. Joe grabbed the person by his hair and almost literally threw him down the stair. The person stopped rolling near the bottom of the stair and crawled away before Joe could get to him. Instead of an arthritis flareup keeping Mr. Johns home for a few days, what he heard this time was that Mr. Johns might miss the remainder of the year. Joe grinned about that, but he didn't think it meant SueAnn would be safe from the creep. He also couldn't think who the man and woman might be that Flex saw poking through the ashes of his former home. He knew very well who Tim Klein was, the man, both Flex Cheney and Ray Feinberg, warned him about. Tim Klein didn't happen to be a teacher at IHS, so he'd be harder to keep track of; he didn't know if there were more threats out there or not.

SueAnn took her own car to school on Tuesday and dropped in on her old roommate Jan after school. Jan had a tendency to be pessimistic and sad; SueAnn felt a mission to help lighten her up. But on Tuesday, Jan was already light—even bubbly. SueAnn and Jan went through college together and started at IHS at the same time. They'd been roommates since they graduated and had much giggling and catching up to do. But SueAnn remembered why she'd come after a little over an hour, and looked intently at Jan. "May I ask you a favor?"

Jan gave a radiant smile, and answered, "Of course, SueAnn. After I ask one of you."

"What is it?"

"Will you be the matron of honor at my wedding to Tom?"

That question set off another round of squeals and giggles, but fewer this time. "Oh, Jan. If you love Tom now, it will only become more intense after you're married. I can hardly wait to grow old with Joe, and perhaps even have our boys take care of us, instead of the other way around."

SueAnn saw a hint of the old glum look pass over Jan's face. "You might not make it, SueAnn. Clifford or Stella might make sure you don't."

SueAnn searched her memory but came up with nothing. "Clifford? Stella?" Jan's gloomy look became more obvious. "Let me jog your memory.

Biology class at Texas Tech." SueAnn searched once more and again could only think of the same nothing.

She did recall biology, a class she hated, taught by a woman she didn't like. But she could not call the woman's name to mind, so again, "Clifford? Stella?"

"Oh, you remember. Stella, Dr. Wyman. She taught our biology class, and Stella's married to Clifford."

SueAnn did faintly remember the name, Dr. Wyman. She gave a weak smile and went on to her real reason to visit Jan. "Does Tom still work as a magician at children's parties?"

"Yes! He does, and he's always looking for more bookings."

"I plan a birthday party for my sons, Robby and Junior, Saturday, April the twentieth. Is Tom available for that?"

"I'm almost positive he is. May I come too?"

"Of course, you can come. I hope you will." SueAnn hadn't even thought about Jan, but if Jan wanted to attend, SueAnn wanted that too. "Will you call me tonight and confirm the date?"

"Of course."

After some more talk about weddings and birthdays, SueAnn went home. Joe waited to take the boys out to play; they did that, and while the boys played, SueAnn mentioned Clifford and Stella to Joe. She later couldn't remember if she called Stella by that name, or if she identified her as Dr. Wyman. Whichever, Joe seemed to appreciate the information.

Jan called, confirmed the twentieth, and SueAnn felt pleased.

Joe and SueAnn went to school Wednesday morning. Joe made a perfunctory check of SueAnn's room and his own, as he normally did, although he knew Jake wouldn't be in school, and so didn't expect trouble. However, just as he sat at his desk, he heard SueAnn scream. He kicked over a desk and bloodied his shin, but still made it into SueAnn's classroom in record time.

She pointed at a note on her desk. "Jake's out. I'm in. Sweet dreams. (A fellow teacher.) She whispered, "Who could it be, Joe?"

Chapter 9

Smithson Reiland

Joe looked. He whispered back, "I don't know." He folded the note and put it in his shirt pocket.

Joe returned to his classroom. He set the desk back up he'd kicked over, and noted the blood he'd felt had become visible. He wondered who Jake's replacement could be. He didn't want to rule out women, but did, as he thought about who might take Jake's place. Not a lot of men teachers remained; he thought of a couple vocational teachers—Smithson Rielend, Vo-Ag teacher, and Edgar Winegarten, shop teacher. He went to the school office to learn when each had a free period. Rielend's was first hour, and Winegarten's, sixth hour. He decided to check on Edgar Winegarten first. He trotted out to the shop building before school and saw Winegarten at his desk. He sat quietly until Joe had to go back to his own class. After class, Joe ran out to the Vo-Ag building. Smithson happened to not be in the building, so Joe rummaged around in his desk and in the shop. He didn't find anything, but Mr. Rielend found him, as he closed a cabinet door in the shop. Rielend entered the building, stopped, looked, and asked, in a disapproving tone, "May I help you?"

Joe jumped. He then fished around in his shirt pocket, found the note, walked to the door, showed the note to Smithson, and asked, "You ever see this?"

"Where'd you find it?" Joe thought perhaps the impassive look on Smithson's face slipped a bit.

He tried to memorize everything about Mr. Rielend, from the manure on his oxfords, to his jeans, to his apparently home-made silver belt buckle, to his plaid shirt, including his little pig eyes, his off-center piggish snout (his nose and mouth seemed too far right, and with other characteristics, they made him think of a pig snout) all the way to the reading glasses on his head and to the braid behind the glasses. Joe thought maybe he'd been too critical. He searched Smithson's face for an attractive feature but could find none, except for his Adam's apple, which seemed normal and in a normal place. But his Adam's apple didn't seem to be a part of his face, and anyway, his eyes kept drifting to the pig snout look. He could almost see himself grab the braid in back and whirl the guy like he had a snake by the tail. "Uh...I thought maybe you'd know." Rielend's right hand slipped up to rest on a tire wrench. He said, "If I do, it's none of your business." Joe allowed Smithson to know he saw the hand by flicking his eyes to it, then back to Rielend's face. He pushed the note closer to Rielend, who grabbed it with his left hand and threw it to the floor. Joe left the building and went to see SueAnn.

On the assumption someone might be listening, Joe whispered to SueAnn, "I might have learned something today. I'll tell you about it on the way home."

She whispered back, "OK."

As they drove home later, by a new route, Joe told SueAnn all that'd happened with Smithson Rielend. She wondered, "Do you suppose he'll show up in my class tomorrow?"

"Your first-hour class is small, isn't it?"

"Yes, the first row is empty—I won't let anyone sit there—and only boys who've volunteered, sit in the second row."

"Great. I expect Rielend to show up in your first-hour class tomorrow. I'll warn Pete Wesson in my class, you can speak to the boys in your class, and we'll all jump on him if he shows."

They continued home and found nobody except people who belonged there. So, the next morning, everybody waited for Smithson Rielend to arrive. He didn't disappoint them. About 7:40 am, Joe saw Pete run across the hall, heard SueAnn scream, along with what sounded like every girl in her class, and Joe followed Pete out. He got through his door just in time to see Pete and a couple other boys wrestle Rielend into the hall and push him down the stair. Smithson only fell about five steps and crawled back up. Joe couldn't believe that Rielend would make himself as easy a target as he appeared to. Joe pulled his right leg back to kick and waited. When Rielend was exactly the right distance away, Joe kicked him full in the face and put all his leg strength into the kick. He kicked Smithson back down the stair, but early in his fall, he grabbed Joe's right foot. Joe managed to stay upright for two steps, by hopping down the stairs on his left leg, after Smithson. But then he both felt and heard his leg break. SueAnn covered her mouth in horror, then sent Max Arthurs, one of her students, to bring Mr. Hinkle. Pete Wesson ran down the steps and jumped on a motionless Mr. Rielend. John Hinkle showed up and sent Max back to the office to tell June to call an ambulance for Joe and to call the police about Mr. Rielend. He called down to Pete, "Stay on em' son if you can."

Pete called back, "It's easy sir. He's out cold." He remained atop Mr. Rielend until the police came. They handcuffed Rielend and called a second ambulance. The ambulances took both Joe and Smithson to Methodist Hospital, where doctors told Joe he might be able to return to work, on crutches, in about three weeks if Mr. Hinkle would give him a first-floor room. They told Smithson he'd need reconstructive surgery, and it could be as long as six weeks before he could return. But a police officer told him ten to twenty years might be more realistic.

When doctors stopped working on Joe's leg and put him into a room, SueAnn came there almost instantly. She said, "Mr. Hinkle gave me the rest of the day off. Does your leg hurt terribly?"

"It hurts, but I can't say 'terribly.'"

"Did they say when you can come back?"

"Yeah, maybe in about three weeks, if Hinkle lets me have a first-floor room."

"That'll be the first thing I work on tomorrow. There's a music room on the first floor, at the north end of the building. And an art room adjacent. I won't let you go alone. I'll insist I go too."

"That ought to work because I'll insist on the same thing!"

Chapter 10

Stella and Clifford Wyman

Joe's leg improved, and he could have gone back to work after three weeks. But he asked for three more days. He intended to use the time to check out the Wyman's and Tim Klein. He chose Stella, the biology professor, to be first. He found she had a class about to begin when he arrived at the University, so he went in the biology auditorium, found a chair on the back row, and sat. He arranged his crutches alongside and prepared to stay awake.

About halfway through her lecture, he noted that she spoke sharply to a black student, but then he noticed she spoke sharply to everyone, so maybe his early observation didn't mean anything. Near the end of the lecture, he realized how different his appearance was from that of the other students and wondered if she knew him. However, the lecture had almost ended, and if she'd recognized him, it was too late to worry about it. Next, he sat outside the biology building in his truck, all the rest of the day. She came out about half-past five, got in a car with some guy, and Joe tailed the car to a house in Lubbock, at the address he'd looked up that morning for her and her husband. The car went into the garage at the house there. Her behavior seemed so normal as to be downright boring. He wasn't sure he had anything to worry about with Stella.

He designated the next day Clifford Wyman day. He'd learned that Stella's husband had a real estate office in downtown

Lubbock. He drove to the office, parked a block away on the street, and watched all day. The guy—the same one he'd seen drive Dr. Wyman to her home—drove his car to an upscale Lubbock restaurant with a couple—possibly clients- remained there from eleven fifty-five am to one-twenty pm, came back alone, went to the biology building about half-past five, and picked up Dr. Wyman again. About as unexceptional and boring as the doctor herself.

His experience with Tim Klein, except for one thing he did, bored him as well. Tim, a building contractor, occupied a suite in a big building in Idalou. Joe tailed him all day; Tim drove around and visited various building sites. In the one behavior, Joe thought could mean something, Tim drove past Joes burned house, and slowed as he went by. Joe thought the fact he tried to make something of that in his mind perhaps only proved paranoia. But then Joe thought, if anybody had reason to be paranoid, it was him. In the end, he didn't think he'd learned anything at all about Tim, or the other two either.

Joe went back to school, but nothing sinister happened for a few weeks. Two interesting things happened during those weeks, however. One, the judge in Rielend's trial let him off. And second, Joe made another trip out to Ransom Canyon and found Ralph had moved—to Idalou, to the house between his old, burned one, and the house owned by Roy, Helen's dad. Joe didn't understand why Ralph chose that house to buy, but he thought it might be bad.

Joe hobbled for a while, but no more notes or attacks came until after the birthday party, so both Joe and SueAnn were free to concentrate on the party, scheduled for April 20, Saturday.

Joe's dad, Joseph, Sr., wrote to accept the invitation to the party and to say he'd come a couple of days earlier. His letter arrived on April 2. SueAnn waved the letter around like a trophy.

Her parents, John and Sylvia, also wrote to accept; their letter arrived on April fifteen; they said they'd show up during the evening of the nineteenth. SueAnn acted pleased they could attend, but her pleasure seemingly didn't match that when she learned Joe's dad would be there.

When he arrived, she ran out to his car with arms open wide for a hug. Joseph, however, looked busy lighting a cigarette, so she folded her arms at the last minute in a manner she felt probably made her look foolish. Joe found a way to be busy in the backyard and came in the back door about ten minutes after Joseph came through the front. Joseph asked for help getting his bags inside; he looked.so frail, SueAnn encouraged Joe to go out and help, so Joe went. While outside, Joseph asked if he could stay with Joe and SueAnn for at least a year.

Joe shook his head no and then elaborated. "Your smoking and drinking'll set a bad example for Junior and Robby. They don't need that."

"What if I quit—cold turkey?"

"You can't do it. You quit today, then come back in a couple of months. I'll think about it then. But not now, because I know you won't do it."

"I will do it. And you can hold me to it. Please, Joe. I can't take much more of the loneliness I've had in Post."

Joe shook his head no again, then said he'd see what SueAnn thought. He took two bags in the house, maintained his dark visage, and found SueAnn. "Dad wants to stay with us for a while. What's your opinion?"

"Oh, Joel I hope you fell all over him with yesses. He needs a family. Please tell me you said yes!"

"I didn't. He claims he'll stop drinking and smoking if he stays."

"Joe, that's an answer to my prayers. Run right back out there and say yes!" "You know he won't."

"Won't what?" "Stop.

"Joe!" She grinned at him and slapped his forearm. "We must give him a chance. What kind of faith do I exhibit if we don't?"

Joe moved toward the front door, but said over his shoulder, "Realistic faith."

He walked back out to where Joseph still stood, by the trunk of his car. "SueAnn says yes."

"Joseph, Sr.'s grin stretched all the way across his face. "You won't regret it Son. I'll be the best grandpa those boys could want—you could want for them."

"We'll see. If I come home from school one time, and smell cigarette smoke, or find a liquor bottle in the trash—and I'll look—you're outta here."

Joseph's grin didn't waver. "You won't, Son. I've already quit."

Joe picked up the third and last bag, still with his grim look. "Right. And if you haven't, I'll kick you all the way back to Post."

Joe kept the mood strained until five forty-five the next day when John and Sylvia Thomas showed up. They looked so healthy, relative to Joseph that Robby asked his parents about it. "How come Grandpa, and Grandma Thomas are as young as you guys, but Grandpa Alley is so old?"

Joe's countenance went dark, but SueAnn answered. "Grandpa Alley is actually about two years younger than your other grandparents, but he's had a harder life." She didn't want him to understand, and he didn't. He made a halfhearted effort to pretend he did.

John and Sylvia added a needed jovial note to the group, and everyone's mood lifted. They all went to bed early, because they knew the boys would be excited and up early on Saturday. Joseph Sr. slept in the spare room, Joe and SueAnn slept on a pallet in the living room, and John and Sylvia slept in the so-called master bedroom.

The day of the party arrived plenty slowly, in the minds of Junior and Robby, but it eventually came. All the people SueAnn had invited were there, plus about half the kids in Idalou, according to Joe's estimate. Junior and Robby had a great time, but the grandparents almost as great. Tom Braque, Jan Evans' boy-friend—er fiancé—was a hit as a magician, but the day ended, and everyone except Joseph Sr. went home. SueAnn exhaled a sigh of relief. She'd wanted the party, and thought it a success, but was now glad to have it over. They didn't take the boys away from home to play on Saturday because of the party, or on Sun-day because they still thought of Joseph Sr. as a guest.

They all, including Joseph, Sr., went to church on Sunday, and all enjoyed it, even Joe.

Joe allowed the mood to lift a bit, and even said to his dad, "I thought you'd be off the wagon by now, and although I still don't think you can hold out indefinitely, I'm impressed you lasted this long." Joseph didn't reply.

Joe and SueAnn talked Sunday night after Joseph retired for the night. One of SueAnn's topics was Joseph. "He's done so great. I even think maybe he looks a little healthier. What do you think?"

"Yeah, maybe. You have any ideas on how can we get the goods on Ralph Johnson?"

"I'm not as interested in Ralph Johnson as I am Joseph. And although you act like you are, I know you're not."

On the way home from church, SueAnn had asked, "How long do you think we should wait before we replace Jim Crane with your dad?"

"That's a dumb notion, SueAnn. Dad couldn't hold off a female field mouse."

SueAnn grinned and slapped Joe's forearm. "Oh, Joe, you know he could. And he looks stronger every day! Jim's still stronger, but Joseph loves the boys. I'm ready to dump Jim today."

"Well, I'm not, and I don't want to talk about it. Not now, not ever."

"Maybe Jim'd let Joseph use his squirrel rifle."

"I said I don't want to talk about it."

SueAnn smiled. "OK Joe, but expect me to pester you about it about every day until you give up."

Joe mumbled and grumped. Then he asked, "Since you don't want to talk about Ralph, you got any ideas on how we can trap Tim Klein?"

"Joseph had a suggestion last week. You want to hear about it?"

"I asked you if you had an idea."

"I don't. But I do have a thought about Clifford."

"What?"

"Maybe we could persuade Beth to call him and say she wants to sell this house. Ask him to come and look. Perhaps he'll say something he shouldn't when he's around the boys." "Maybe.

Will you set it up?"

"Of course, Joe."

They resumed the normal habit of taking the boys out to play, beginning Monday after the party, but switched from the truck to SueAnn's car, because three adults and two boys crowded a pickup cab.

The following Wednesday evening at 5:30 sharp, Clifford of Wyman and Roberts Realty, showed up at Beth's house, occupied by Joe, the twins, Joseph, and SueAnn. Clifford rang the doorbell and looked like he might be about to bolt when SueAnn opened the door. He didn't run, but went through the door and into the house, and then seemed businesslike and professional while inside; he said he'd soon let them know what he thought the house would sell for as he left. Even though SueAnn had prepped the boys to stay close to him, he said nothing to incriminate himself.

After Clifford had gone, SueAnn looked at Joe. "Well, that was a bust."

"Yep. You got any more thoughts?"

"No."

Thursday morning at school, Klaus Simpson, Joe's third-hour big boy in the corner, suddenly began to repeatedly jab his thumb toward the hallway, and soon after, everybody could hear a bunch of screaming in SueAnn's room. Joe tried to enter her room right behind Klaus but was almost knocked down by a man running out of the room, wearing a cape and a mask.

"You got any notion who that was?" Joe looked perplexed.

SueAnn looked perplexed too, but said, "Maybe...Clifford... Wyman? Whoever it was, he's about Clifford's size and wore the same kind of shoes Clifford wore yesterday."

"But that isn't much to go on. How about Tim Klein? Is he bigger or smaller, and what kind of shoes does he wear?"

"Both guys might be about average. And I don't have a clue about Tim's shoes. You ever see anybody in your room wear a cape before? Coach Bolivan had one in his office, but as far as I know, he never wore it."

"No."

"Let's go on the assumption the guy was Clifford Wyman. If we do that, you think we can get him back? If that happens, maybe I can get over here sooner next time."

"Maybe you or Joseph could pretend to want to see houses. He saw you both at Beth's house yesterday."

Joe scowled. "That would be me. I'm not going to let my dad take that kind of risk."

SueAnn grinned and slapped Joe's forearm. "Joe! You sound almost protective of your dad!"

Joe's scowl deepened, then went away. He grinned. "Maybe I am. Or maybe it's because of Claude. He says if anything happens to the old man, he'll kill me!"

SueAnn grinned then. "Are you afraid of your brother, Joe? How embarrassed you must feel! He's at least ten years older than you, a foot shorter, and has at least twenty extra pounds on his belly!"

"He's only eight years older."

"He looks ten to twelve more, and he has two sons ten to twelve years older than Robby and Junior."

Joe grinned again. "No, I'm not afraid of Claude. Maybe I am getting protective!"

"Either way, I'll be the one to look at houses with Clifford. Can you set it up?"

"I could, but it might seem more authentic to him if you did."

"Whatever. I'll do it."

Joe looked at houses with Clifford Wyman on Saturday. He glommed onto a couple of ideas to incorporate into his own home when he got around to rebuilding it but didn't catch Clifford in anything.

He and SueAnn talked about his efforts later on Saturday. "I'm not sure Clifford's our guy, SueAnn. He acted normal all day, I thought."

"Who else, then?"

"Tim Klein?"

SueAnn didn't answer, and the conversation turned another direction. Sunday morning, in SueAnn's Sunday School class, though, they saw a message on a dry-erase board that had to be from Clifford. The message read, 'I'll not sell a house for anybody that associates with a lover of blacks, and I'll not act as broker for anybody like that. The only thing I'll do for you is get rid of the two kids for you.'

SueAnn had both pen and paper; she copied the note, and on the way home, she and Joe talked about it. "What can we do to protect the boys, Joe?"

Joe shook his head. "I dunno, SueAnn."

"How about if we warn Jim Crane, and ask Joseph to stay in the room with the boys and make sure they stay quiet?"

"The Jim Crane part's OK, but Dad's no force."

"No force!? I might have to paddle you, Joe!" Joseph grinned as he said it, but also straightened his shoulders, flexed his right bicep, and tried to look tough.

"It won't hurt anything, though, will it?" SueAnn didn't give up.

"All you plan to ask of him is that he keeps the boys quiet?"

"Yes."

"He probably can't do it, but no, it shouldn't hurt."

"Thanks, Joe. I'll take care of it all. I'll warn Jim, and check again with Joseph."

"I could stay home if you think I should."

SueAnn laughed and slapped Joe's forearm. "And leave me unprotected at school? I don't think so!"

SueAnn and Joe went to school on Monday, but nothing happened there. They came home after school, to find Jim sitting on the front porch, with his squirrel rifle across his knees. He looked relaxed and comfortable, Joe exhaled a sigh of relief, opened the truck door for SueAnn, and walked her toward Jim. Jim looked at them, almost with amusement in his eyes, and said, "You guys missed all the excitement."

Joe suddenly tensed up. "What excitement?"

"Go on in and see the dead man in your boys' room."

Joe forgot about SueAnn and almost stepped on Jim as he ran through the open front door. He planned to continue running, right on into the twins' room, but tripped-over a person—a dead person—just inside the door. He fell flat, then looked up to see six very serious eyes look at him from the other side of the boys' bed. "What happened here," he asked.

Robby answered. "A bad man came in. He said he'd kill Junior and me. Grandpa hit the man on the head with a lamp, and he died."

Joe laboriously got to his feet. He slowly walked around the bed and hugged—Joseph! Then he hugged Junior and Robby while saying, "Dad, you're the hero here. I take my hat off to you"—he didn't because he wasn't wearing a hat- "and can't tell you how glad I am you're here. You got a place here as long as you want it." Robby and Junior hugged Joseph's legs. All four—including Joe—had wide grins on their faces. They all four stepped over the dead person again and went outside to tell SueAnn what had happened.

SueAnn had an immediate question, "Is the dead guy Clifford?"

Junior and Robby both nodded yes.

"Then I must call Stella."

Joe almost ran to get between SueAnn and the telephone. "Wait, SueAnn. We need to call the police first."

SueAnn shook her head. "I'll call the police immediately after I call Stella, but I must call her first." She made the calls in that order, then looked at Joe. "Stella threatened me, Joe. She somehow thinks it's my fault that Clifford is dead."

"How specific is her threat?"

"The threat is awfully specific. She says she'll kill ME. But she doesn't say when."

"Maybe that's good. We don't have to figure out how to find her that way."

"You might think it's good, Joe, but I don't!"

"I didn't mean it that way SueAnn, but whatever, we'll see her when we see her. Who wants to go to Uncle Claude's to play?"

Junior answered enthusiastically. "Yay! I do!"

Robby added, "Me too!"

All five (SueAnn, Joe, Joseph, Junior, and Robby) crowded into SueAnn's car, and soon everybody piled out at Claude's; Claude joined them, and everybody had a great time for almost an hour. Then they heard two rifle shots, and SueAnn went down. Blood poured from her head and her chest area. Three of the four went to her instantly but fell back when Joe arrived. He held her in his arms and tried to pray. He said, "God, please don't let her die. Please, please let her live; let her be like she's always been."

Joe looked up, and said, "She needs to get to a doctor quick. Let's go to Chapman Clinic again. Joe knew his prayer skill was pathetic, but he tried again as he drove, all the way to the Clinic. He heard the boys and Joseph doing the same; Joe drove faster than the speed limit, and the trip didn't last long. Dr. Chapman took one look and said she looked bad. He worried about both death, and about brain damage. And said he couldn't guarantee anything. Joe redoubled his attempts at prayer when he heard Dr. Chapman's pessimism.

Dr. Chapman shook his head, then said, "She needs to be in a hospital." Joe moved to lift her back into the car, but Dr. Chapman shook his head again. "I'll call an ambulance." He did, and minutes later, medics put her into it. Joe asked Dr. Chapman what hospital he'd specified; Dr. Chapman said, "The closest one: Methodist. So, all four guys jumped back in the Falcon and raced over to Methodist, where her ambulance bypassed another, and she was taken in immediately, on a stretcher.

Joe didn't bother to park the car but merely stopped. He, his dad, and his sons jumped out and followed SueAnn inside. Every doctor who saw her looked grave; they eventually installed her in a room. All four guys followed, and Joe continued his prayer effort. After a while, Joe asked Joseph to take the boys home and said he planned to stay all night. He clung to the belief she'd be all right by morning. But she wasn't.

Morning came, and SueAnn remained unconscious. Joe called Mr. Hinkle, told him what had happened and that he planned to stay with SueAnn all day, or longer if necessary. Except for an occasional nap in a chair by her bedside, and an occasional drink from a water fountain just outside her room, Joe didn't eat, drink, or sleep for five days. Joseph and the boys visited twice, and Joseph urged him to go home and rest, but he refused. He continued to "pray without ceasing." Eventually, on the afternoon of the fifth day, Saturday, SueAnn opened her eyes. She looked groggy and didn't ask how long she'd been there, but Joe took it as answered prayer. Joe told her he loved her, she smiled and closed her eyes again. Joe went home fell into his bed and awoke Sunday morning. He ate more breakfast than a lumberjack should eat, told Joseph his good news, and returned to the hospital. SueAnn was awake and had also eaten a few bites when he arrived! He continued to "pray without ceasing," but he switched to prayers of thanks. He told SueAnn, "I'm not positive that I know who shot you, but I assume it was Clifford's wife, and I'll hunt her down and kill her."

SueAnn frowned. "Joe, that's wrong. I don't want you to do it."

"It doesn't matter what you want. I'll do it anyway."

"Please don't. I've been lying here thanking God for my life. If I allow you to take Stella's life-and I think of you as part of me-what will that do to my relationship with God?"

"You really think there's a connection?"

"I know there is, Joe."

Joe shook his head as if to clear it. Then, after a silent moment, "I prayed constantly you'd make it, SueAnn. You think God will take you away if I kill Stella?"

"No, Joe, I don't think that, but I do think it will be a deliberate backing away from God. I don't want to do that, and I hope you don't either."

"I don't. If I had my hands around her throat, I'd...remove them! Did Dr. Chatman say when you can come home?"

"No, I haven't asked him."

"We all want you home! Ask him! I'm not going to take any chance that whoever shot you at Claude's will be at Lubbock High. I plan to build a concrete block wall around Beth's backyard, so the boys can play out there each day, under Dad's supervision. If Beth doesn't like it, I'll tear it down when we leave, but whether she likes it or not, it will stay until people stop hating you, or until we leave. And the boys will have to keep on staying inside until I get it built. They'll be willing; they've already proposed we stop our earlier routine. They seem as worried about your safety as I am! I'll get to work on the wall today." Joe jumped up from SueAnn's bedside and almost ran away. He had the wall completed, except for the south end, by Sunday evening. He told Joseph he'd finish on Monday, but he could take the boys out anyway if he made sure they stayed near the north end of the backyard. Joe said he'd return to school on Monday. The boys played in the backyard, with no incident on Monday.

SueAnn called Joseph Monday and told him Dr. Chapman had cleared her to leave the hospital that evening but hadn't cleared her to go back to school. According to SueAnn, Dr. Chapman told her not to go back to school until he said it was OK; he said he wouldn't tell her to go back for at least several weeks, probably not until fall of the next school year. Joe, his dad, and the twins all went to fetch her from the hospital before Joe began again on the wall. They had to wait for a while, and it took more time to help SueAnn get settled in bed, so Joe did nothing on the wall that evening, but waited until Tuesday, the last day of April. Although he finished in the dark, he did complete the wall that day.

When he had the wall all done, he ran into the house, to see SueAnn. His dad and sons already sat by her bedside. Joe arrived as she ended a tirade about Joseph's glasses. "And they make you look old, as if you made them yourself, and used baling wire and window glass." When Joe sat down by her bed, she turned to him. "Your glasses are barely better. Did you make them in the dark...with your eyes closed? You both need to get new ones-and better ones—as fast as you can." Then she looked at the boys. "You boys need a haircut and a style. You look like your hair fell out of the sky on your heads. Likewise, for your dad and your grandfather." She rolled over in bed and faced the wall, to signify the conversation had ended.

Robby, with a hurt look, said to Joe, "I thought you said she's like a mom oughta be. SueAnn rolled back to face Robby, and said, "Oh Robby, that's exactly what I want to be. If I sounded harsh...and I know I did...I'm sorry. I'd been holding that back for so long, I know it came out wrong...terrible. Can you forgive me?"

An uncertain grin slowly spread over Robby's face. He glanced at Joe, who gave him an almost imperceptible yes nod. His grin suddenly looked fully authentic, but he only said, "Sure, Mom."

SueAnn smiled. "You do need to do something about your hair, though. Your father and grandfather do too, along with their glasses. Maybe you can influence those older guys?"

Robby's grin held as he looked around at his dad, grandpa, and at Junior. "Sure, Mom."

Joe didn't receive more threats during SueAnn's hospitalization, but Wednesday, April 24, he received new information. Principal Hinkle told him someone with a male voice at a Tuesday night board meeting called SueAnn a "black lover," and called Joe a "lover of a black lover." Mr. Hinkle said he sat near the front, and the person he quoted sat in back, so he didn't know who said it, and couldn't describe the person. Joe's opinion of John Hinkle dropped even lower than it had already been. Joe didn't know if the speaker had been Clifford, Tim Klein, or somebody else. After he considered various strategies, he decided to work down his existing list of suspects, and worry later about whether or who to add to the list. He decided to try to trap Ralph Johnson first. So, Wednesday evening, he knocked on Ralph's door. A short, chubby, bald, middle aged man wearing a business suit answered the door. Joe asked, "May I come in?"

The man asked, "First of all, who are you?"

Joe responded, "I'm Joe Alley, your next-door neighbor." The man slammed the door. Joe mentally firmed up Ralph's position on his list of suspects and began to think about ways to get him out of his house. After a moment he went to a back tire of Ralph's car, unscrewed the valve core, and allowed the core to blow out on the driveway. His reward was the sound of escaping air, followed by a flat tire. He considered also banging a rock on the man's car trunk but dropped that idea as a likely step toward jail. Instead of banging the rock, he went back home and watched Ralph's house. After about fifty minutes Mr. Johnson came out of his house, started the car, and started to drive away. He soon parked beside the road, looked at his tires, and stopped by the flat one. Joe walked to the spot, and said, "Need any help?"

"Not from the likes of you."

"Want to come in and use my telephone?"

The man didn't answer, so Joe asked, "Do you know Edith Wyatt?"

The man again didn't answer, so Joe moved behind a tree in Beth's yard and asked, "Did you shoot Mrs. Wyatt?"

Ralph not only didn't answer, but he also bolted for his front door. Joe ran to stand in front of it, and asked again, "Did you shoot Mrs. Wyatt?"

Still no answer. Joe said, "I know you did. You might as well go on down to the police station and turn yourself in."

Finally, Ralph answered, "In your dreams."

Joe sighed and returned to his home. Although he hadn't gotten a confession, he thought he knew for sure Ralph had killed Mrs. Wyatt. He beckoned to one of Beth's' guards.' The 'guard' came near, and he told him what had happened. The 'guard' shook his head. "We can't do nothin' long as the guy stays in his house. But we'll watch. If 'e gets too close to your house, we'll jump em.'"

Joe hoped the guy'd try an attack at school, while SueAnn wasn't there. Nothing happened at school on Thursday, but when Joe came home, Joseph told him he'd made appointments for them both to get new spectacles that evening. They went, and SueAnn said the new ones looked a hundred percent better. Nothing happened at the school Friday either, but Jim Crane claimed he shot at Ralph that day, but missed. Joe hid up in a front yard tree before daylight and waited. He almost came down about half past eight, but the Johnson house lights went on, so he decided to wait longer. Fatigue almost drove him down again, at about ten o'clock, but Ralph came outside then and approached Joe's house. Joe quickly climbed down from the tree, ran up behind Ralph, and asked the same question Ralph had asked him. "May I help you?"

Ralph whirled around, seemed panicked, but recovered, and said, "No thanks."

Saturday morning, Joe, Joseph, and the twins got their hair styled and cut; SueAnn bragged on their looks even more than she had when Joe and his dad changed their glasses. All four guys basked in her approval, especially Junior and Robby.

When they returned from the barber shop, Joe sat in the living room and tried to think who Mr. Hinkle could have overheard at the school board meeting. Nothing came to his mind, so he returned to thinking of a way to trap Ralph Johnson. After a while, he stood, walked purposefully into the kitchen, called The Idalou Beacon, and had them run the following ad for two weeks. "I'm now out of the hospital. To reach me, call me at home, or during school hours 892-6868. Edith Wyatt."

Two days after the ad appeared, the telephone rang at Joe's house. He answered, "Hello."

Roy Wyatt, responded, with an angry sound to his voice. "You Joe Alley?"

"Yes."

"You put the stupid ad in the paper about Edith?"

"Yes."

"You trying to make Helen and me suffer more, are you?"

"No. I'm hoping the real killer will show up here again or will call."

"Yeah, right." Click.

Joseph asked, "Who was that?"

Joe's face showed concern. "It was Roy Wyatt. I put an ad in the Beacon, purporting to be by Edith Wyatt, in an effort to get Ralph Johnson to either come here or to call. Roy thinks it's to add to his suffering."

Joseph's face mirrored Joe's concern. "You need to go over there, Son, and make him understand," Joe argued with his dad about the futility of such a visit and didn't go.

The remainder of the two weeks passed, plus another, and except for Roy, no one called. Joe tried to think of another plan. He decided to try to organize a neighborhood "fix-up" for the widow lady who lived across the street from Ralph Johnson. He talked to several people in his neighborhood, and to Helen at school. He thought enough time had passed that Helen might tell him what she knew. Because he'd decided to go through with the "fix-up," regardless of what Helen told him, he left the pressing question for last. After he explained his "fix-up" plans, to include yard work in the lady's lawn, repair of her non-running car, various furniture-refinishing projects in front of the house she lived in, plus some cleaning in the lady's house, and told her of the date, Saturday, May 4, weather permitting, he asked, "Will you come, and will you invite your and your Uncle Ralph come?"

A doubtful look crossed Helen's face. "I think my dad won't, and he'll probably not allow me to go either, although I will if he gives the OK"

"What about your Uncle Ralph?" "I know sure he won't."

"Well, I suppose I can live with that if you'll tell me who killed Edith."

A fearful look settled on her face then and didn't go away. "I don't dare tell you that."

"Thanks, Helen. Drop over and say hello to the boys Saturday, or any day you choose. And I won't ask you there who killed your mom, OK?"

"I'll be there as soon as my dad says I can."

Joe did the "fix-up" day on May 4 but still didn't see Ralph Johnson or anyone else he thought dangerous, so he tried again on May 11, with a neighborhood dinner. SueAnn was sometimes up by that day, but Joe didn't want to ask her to cook yet, so bought a chocolate pie and fried chicken at a local grocery-caterer. As on the previous Saturday, no one Joe thought of interest showed up.

The last day of school happened on the following Thursday, May eighteenth. Because no one appeared in Joe's classroom that day, or any day in May, he knew someone could show up at his home during the summer. Indeed, he went home from school on the eighteenth and found trouble. When he arrived at home, he saw Jim Cline sit outside by the front door, with his squirrel gun over his legs. He sent Jim home and went inside. He went first to SueAnn's room, said hello to her, and went next to his sons' room. Among the first things he saw, however, was something he thought might be a cannon barrel (actually it was a pistol barrel) stuck through the boys' window. He spoke in a low voice, but the boys correctly interpreted his words as a command, "Get in Mom's room, quick." The pistol barrel adjusted until Joe thought he could see all the way inside it to the very back of it, including a bullet back there with his name written on it. Joe fell to the floor, heard the roar of the gun, heard something break, saw a hole appear in the ceiling above him, and felt some ceiling texture fall on him. He carefully and slowly raised himself to his hands and knees, hid behind the bed as he crawled to the foot of it, then crawled as fast as he could to the wall beside the window, then slowly stood to look out the window. The pistol had gone away. He saw an unconscious person face down on the lawn outside, with a broken lamp nearby, and also saw Joseph hurry through the back door into the house. He ran out of the boys' room, and into the room Joseph had entered. Joseph locked the door, turned, and saw Joe. He said, "Ralph Johnson tried to break into the boys' room. I hit em' with a lamp. He might not still be alive, but in any case, we need to get the police here."

Joe agreed, went to the kitchen, and used the telephone to call the police. They arrived and pronounced Ralph dead. Two officers arrived and took a statement from Joseph. As they left, one mentioned how many times they'd found some kind of a crime at Joe's place; the other grinned, and said, "I never want to meet your dad and a lamp in a dark place named after you, Joe Alley!"

After Joe's mind processed what had happened, he breathed a sigh of relief. But his relief was only momentary because he realized Dr. Wyman, Tim Klein, and possibly any number of others remained out there. He also wondered how Ralph had gotten into his backyard, and if Robby and Junior were as safe out there as he'd thought. He couldn't expect people to show up at school, couldn't expect help from Pete Wesson or anybody in his classes, and didn't know if the remaining people'd merely give up, or would try to attack him, SueAnn, or their boys at home. As he continued to think about the problem, he concluded he needed to try to trap Dr. Wyman first-because SueAnn might know something about her-then Tim Klein-and if anyone else remained, maybe they'd make themselves obvious. He did take the precaution of buying three baseball bats, one for Joseph and one each for SueAnn and for him.

Later that day, he asked SueAnn, "What do you know about Professor Wyman?"

"Practically nothing, except she seemed to rub me the wrong way a bit."

"Maybe I've learned more than that. She's 41 years old, a widow-she was married to Clifford, but he's recently dead, as you know. Do you know where she shopped, ate, or who she hung out with?"

"No. She did like coffee; there was a vending machine down the hall from the Biology Auditorium, and I saw her there a few times-she always had a cup on the demonstration bench as she taught."

"Hm. That is not much to go on. Maybe I'll go to the biology department at a time when I know she's teaching and ask a few questions. He went into the biology office, at ten am, and found some biology professors there. He gave his name, address, and place of employment, because he wanted Dr. Wyman to know, not just someone, but he, Joe Alley, had been finding out information about her. He asked a few questions, then went home and alerted Jim Cline, the 'guards,' and his dad. But nothing happened that day, or for several days.

As Joe waited for something to happen, he talked to Joseph about the backyard. "Dad, it bothers me that Frank somehow got in the backyard. I went out to look and found what looks like dozens of impressions of ladders in the dirt around the flowers outside the new wall. So, I have an idea. Maybe we can buy a bunch of cattle panels to lean against the wall, run a bare wire behind them that doesn't' touch them, attached to a relay, and when a ladder pushes a cattle panel into the bare wire, the relay will set off an electronic siren. You think that could work?"

"Yes, Son, but probably only one time."

"You could be right. But if you have the boys outside, and the electronic siren goes, get them inside fast, and to the front of the house."

"Will do, Son."

The siren went off the first night, so Joe talked again to his dad. "How about motion sensors attached to an electronic siren?" His dad thought that could also work, but again, probably only one time. Joe agreed but thought it could be interesting to leave the cattle panels in place. The motion sensors detected motion the next night. So, Joe's next proposal was, "What if we put precariously balanced wood flower pots in various places atop the wall, attached to a 2 x 6 all along the wall? If somebody pulls on the 2 x 6 or a flower pot, the whole thing will fall outside the wall and brush the person off the ladder. Or if somebody pushes on any of that, everything will fall inside the wall. If either happens, of course, be sure to get the boys in the house, and at the front."

Nothing happened for a few days and nights but early on Wednesday morning, May 29, Joe awakened to hear a gun cocking sound. He suddenly felt fully awake; the sound reverberated off the walls. He pushed SueAnn off the left side of the bed, even though he knew she hadn't fully healed from her gunshot wounds. As he pushed SueAnn, he fell off the right side of the bed and saw a shadowy form over by the entry door, pulling up a pistol.

He kept rolling when he hit the floor, grabbed the form's ankle, and jerked it. The form turned the lights on with its left hand and shot at him with the right. The ankle jerk, however, messed up the person's aim, revealed by the light to be Professor

Wyman. She pulled up the gun again, but SueAnn, not hurt at all by being pushed out of bed, came running around the foot of the bed and actually jumped over a corner of it, with baseball bat held high, and brought it down as hard as she could on the arm holding the pistol. The pistol fell on the floor and discharged. The arm broke, so much that the broken part hung down vertically from the unbroken part. Either the second gun sound or Stella's scream brought Joseph into the room at a run. He grabbed Stella's left arm with his and twisted it behind her, then put his right arm in a choking position in front of her, and said to Joe, "I got'er and won't let'er loose. You need to call the police, Son."

Joe nodded, but first asked SueAnn, "You all right?" She nodded yes, but added, "I think I'll go back to bed though." Joe ran to the telephone in the kitchen and called the police. They came, took Stella away, and Joseph went back to the guest room-his room. Joe stayed in his room, with SueAnn. Joe frowned as he spoke to her. "You sure you're all right?"

SueAnn smiled as she answered. "Yes, I'm sure. I expected something to break open during all the excitement tonight, but it didn't. I'm tired, but perhaps that's because I'm not in shape. I think I'll start spending more time, as early as tomorrow, out of bed, and will feel better because of it."

"In a way, I'm sorry I pushed you out of bed, but in a way, I'm not. I think Stella intended to shoot you as you slept."

Although it remained dark, and Joe couldn't see the grin on SueAnn's face, it was there. She said, "No offense taken THIS TIME, but it had better not EVER happen again. I do still have the bat you know!" They giggled and fell asleep.

They had no more visits until late in July. Saturday night, July twenty seven, SueAnn awakened Joe from a sound sleep. She put her mouth very close to his ear, and whispered softly, "Joe, there's somebody in our room."

Joe, unhappy at being awakened in the middle of the night, opened his eyes and looked around. He became aware of at least two people. He rolled out of bed, grabbed his baseball bat, waved it as though he could see a target, and yelled, "You guys, GET OUT!" He began with a loud voice but hit a crescendo with the final two words. He chased them all the way out the open front door, closed it and locked it, and returned to his bedroom.

SueAnn asked him, "Who were they?"

"There were five of them. I recognized Tim Klein for sure. He looked back, as did one of the others. I'd have said the other person who looked back was Smithson Reilend, from the way he looked from the back, but not so. I've never seen that face before. But I do think I might know who a third person is; I suspect Jake Johns, because he limps, and because he wears a cowboy hat. The other two reminded me of an Erlenmeyer flask we use in the lab at school and a round bottom flask." They smiled.

"Reilend's face might be different, now, after you kicked it." They both giggled.

"I don't think it could be that different. I thought the face halfway average, and that couldn't be Smithson."

"How'd they get in?"

"Apparently through the front door. It was unlocked and open that's how they went out."

"Do you suppose they have a key? That door's often open when somebody's here at night."

"I don't know, SueAnn. Maybe. I can put a chair in front of it, so they'll make noise when they come in."

After some idle chitchat, they went back to sleep. The next morning, instead of a chair, Joe dug a deep hole just inside the front door, with a loud bell to ring if anyone hit the bottom. The very next night, the bell rang. Joe jumped up, found a person he didn't know in the hole, and saw three people running away. He rapped the person in the hole on the head with his bat and knocked him out. Then he went back to his bedroom, and said, "I've never seen the guy in the hole before. Will you come and see if you recognize him? He's the round bottom." SueAnn didn't but called the police. Two officers soon arrived, pulled the awakening intruder out, and looked at his billfold.

"This here guy's driver's license says his name is Otto Best. We don't know him. How'd he get down there?"

Joe explained. The spokesman officer said, "We'll take 'im down to the station, interrogate 'em, run 'is fingerprints, and so on. Maybe we'll learn somthin'."

SueAnn called the next morning to ask what they learned. A person said, "Mr. Best is clean. No record, no nothin'. We let 'im go, but not before he talked about a lawsuit against you folks, for 'indignities suffered.'"

SueAnn reported to Joe. He turned red and answered, "They let...him...go? I wish I'd more than tapped him on the head. I will next time. You still have the police station number?"

"I do, but don't say anything stupid, Joe."

As Joe dialed the number, he said, "I'm sure they'll think what I have to say is stupid. But I don't." When someone at the police station answered, Joe, yelled, "I hope you told that Otto guy to leave us alone. If I get another crack at his head with my bat, I'll do more than tap." The person on the other end of the line began a response, but Joe hung up. Then he strode back and forth in the kitchen a few times. As he did, SueAnn talked.

"So, it appears Otto Best is another one, one we didn't know about before."

"Yeah, it looks that way. And the other three got away again. That gripes me almost as much as Best does. I wonder if June Arlington's heard of Best? I think I'll call her.

Joe returned to the telephone. Then he got sidetracked long enough to look up her number in the book but eventually dialed. "Hi. June there? Can I talk to her please?"

"Hey Joe, how ya doin'?"

"Not so good. You ever hear of a guy named Otto Best?"

"Of course. He's an Alderman, from ward one in Lubbock. He goes by the name Ace."

"Oh, great," Joe explained why he'd called, and they talked a bit more before they hung up. Then he described the phone call to SueAnn.

"Oh, Joe. That might be bad-or good-perhaps the man isn't as stupid as some of the others."

"That only makes him more formidable. But maybe we should forget about him unless he comes back."

"Perhaps, but then who should we focus on?"

"How about we forget them all unless they make a move?"

"We almost know they will, don't we?"

"Yeah, it leaves everything up in the air, but maybe we don't want to look for trouble." He grinned. "We might find it!"

SueAnn looked uncertain. "Well, perhaps."

Joe didn't fill in the hole in front of the door and dug another inside the back door. They laid a heavy board across the hole in front, took it away at night, and didn't use the back door. As Joe hoped, nothing happened for several weeks. Otto Best didn't even bring a lawsuit against them. Joe went back to his routine when school started, however, and asked big strong boys to sit in the corner by the hallway, across from the room SueAnn again occupied. On Monday, September sixteenth, Joe's fifth-hour guy, Robert Barker, suddenly left the room. Then SueAnn and some girls in her room screamed. Joe followed Barker and found Tim Klein-with no mask—facing SueAnn with a knife in his hand. Joe ran into Barker, who'd stopped. Barker then dove for Klein's legs, and Joe grabbed for his knife-wielding arm. Robert missed, Joe missed, and Klein escaped as he ran down the adjacent stairway. Robert tried-and failed-to catch him. A girl in SueAnn's class fainted, and another went for the school nurse; the fainting girl had regained consciousness by the time the nurse arrived, however.

The events of Monday repeated during the second period on Tuesday, except that Tom Wheelock, the big guy in the corner, was absent that day. The first hint of trouble Joe heard was a bunch of screaming from SueAnn's room. As Joe ran into

SueAnn's room, he saw Jake Johns face SueAnn's desk also with no mask, but an even longer and more dangerous looking knife than Tim Klein had displayed. Joe held a half-full beaker in his hand; it contained water, but Joe threw the entire beaker at Jake's eyes, in the hope Jake would think the liquid corrosive. The ploy seemed to work, because Jake pawed at his eyes, and dropped the knife.

Joe grabbed Jake by the neck, and asked, "You want another trip down the stairs?"

He made no move to take Jake to the stairs, but merely held him by the neck, and asked a girl sitting near the middle of the room to go to the office and ask Mr. Hinkley to come. When Hinkley arrived, and after Joe explained, Hinkley said he'd call the police; he asked Joe to continue to hold Johns until the police arrived. The police officers took Jake away, and he didn't bother SueAnn again.

After the Johns episode, Joe kept a beaker half full of water at his desk, to take to future confrontations. They got through Wednesday without a problem, but Thursday, the sixth hour, Joe saw Sean Smith, his big guy in the corner, point across the hall. He soon heard the familiar sound of screams. Joe arrived in the hall just in time to see "the round bottom flask" go around the corner at the bottom of the stair, and disappear.

Friday started with a bang—or a series of bangs. The first-hour bell barely stopped its ring, when someone stuck a pistol inside the door and aimed it at Joe. The big person in the corner, Ed Houser, however, pushed the gun to the right and wrestled the holder of the gun all the way to the front of the room. He grabbed the person by the left arm and twisted it, but the person pointed the pistol at him with his right arm. Ed then grabbed the right arm and tried to turn the pistol toward the shooter, and but slowly, and after some struggle, the pistol ended up pointed down, it went off, and Ed felt the bullet hit his foot-apparently breaking some bones because Ed could feel the ends scrape over one another. He tried to ignore the pain in his foot and banged the shooter's head into the wall, but the head merely broke through the drywall. Ed then moved the man's head to the right and banged it on a two x four stud until the man lost consciousness. Ed turned to hop back to his desk and sit down, but SueAnn came into the room about then. She did a little gasp as she saw the handiwork of the other shooters. Someone had shot from the ceiling, about the middle of the room, and had missed. Someone had shot through a window at the back of the room from Joe's desk and had missed Joe badly, at least 3 feet high and several inches to the right. But someone had shot through the window across from Joe's desk. The bullet grazed his skull along the back, and he was unconscious. Both Ed and SueAnn figured Joe could be dead.

SueAnn looked at Ed and appreciated him, even though she had no idea yet what he'd done-a lot, she presumed. She might even have loved him in a brotherly sort of way. She didn't notice his foot and held out a hand to him. She asked, "Will you hold my hand and stay by me as I go to Joe?"

Ed felt he must say yes, his foot notwithstanding. He held her right hand with his left and touched her back with his right hand. He tried to limp as little as possible as they made their way to the front of the room.

Joe started to regain consciousness before SueAnn and Ed saw him, and by the time they arrived, his eyes were open, and he'd touched his head to try to learn the damage he'd sustained. He looked at SueAnn and smiled. SueAnn threw her arms around him, hugged him, and incoherently said, "Joe! Joe! So glad, Joe!"

Ed didn't see as much as SueAnn did, and tried to get her off Joe, in case she could hurt him. He said, "Maybe you oughtn't to lay on Mr. Alley like that. You might mess up whatever chance he has to get well."

"Look at him,...what is your name?"

"Ed Houser."

"Look at him, Ed. He's good-great-the same old Joe."

"Let me talk to him. Is she right, Mr. Alley?"

"Almost. Something grazed my head, and it hurts. Other than that, she's right.

"Let me look-Oh, wow, I can see bone. But I can't see brains-you're gonna be OK, Mr. Alley."

As further evidence of his recovery, Joe grinned, and joked, "I hope there's a brain somewhere behind the bone!"

Ed turned to SueAnn. I think he's going to be all right, Mrs. Alley. I'll let you at him again!

SueAnn looked at Ed with a question in her eyes. "You think he needs an ambulance?"

"I think he needs to stay on the floor for a while, and you too, until we're sure no more bullets will come." All three of them huddled on the floor, until Ed said, "Maybe that's all there will be. And yes, Mr. Alley needs an ambulance." Ed turned to a nearby student, and asked, "Kay, will you go to the school office and call two ambulances, one for Mr. Alley, and one for me?"

SueAnn looked at Ed, and asked, "Are you injured too?" Ed pointed at his bloody foot.

SueAnn touched it, pulled on his shoelace, and said, "Oh, I'm so sorry. I didn't know you were hurt. Why didn't you say something?"

"P—Please don't touch it. It's killing me."

SueAnn withdrew her hand quickly. "I'm sorry. I didn't know." Then she turned back to Joe and hugged him some more.

Kay came back from the school office and sat again at her desk. They didn't wait very long until they heard a siren. Kay jumped up to show the medics where they needed to go, and they soon arrived. They looked at Joe's head and Ed's foot. The first group took Ed, Mr. Hinkle entered the room, gave SueAnn the day off, and the second bunch took Joe.

SueAnn rode in the ambulance with Joe, but he asked, "How's Ed?"

"Somebody shot him in the foot. He says it hurts, but it has to be nothing compared with what happened to you."

"You might be right, but maybe not. The medics seemed to think his injury is severe-be sure to check on him when we get to the hospital."

"But Joe, I don't want to leave you!"

"It won't take long. You should have seen him take out that... guy."

"You know who that guy is, don't you?"

"Never saw him before in my life."

"The guy is Smithson Rielend."

"His ponytail makes him look that way, but not his face."

"He's had reconstructive surgery on his face, Joe. He was UGLEE, remember? But if you'd kick his face again, the doctors might make him half-way presentable!"

"No. That couldn't have been Smithson."

"It was," SueAnn said it with a definite air of finality, and Joe believed it. Joe changed the subject. He commented that Ed Houser is a senior and on the football team. He followed up with, "Because of his foot, his football career is probably over."

When a doctor visited Joe in the hospital, he minimized his headache. When the doctor asked about it, he said, "It never was too bad, and is gone now." The doctor dismissed Joe, and he went home the same day he arrived. He visited Ed before he went, and Ed told him the doctor said he might be in the hospital at least a week. SueAnn went to school the next day, and Joe showed up in midmorning, to make sure no one bothered her. In both his room and hers, Mr. Hinkle had people about to finish a double wall along the sides of the rooms, the walls about a foot apart, in front of the windows. Joe went to see Mr. Hinkle. "I like the walls. You think they'll stop bullets?"

"I know they will when we finish. The next step will be to put sand between the walls, and a foot of sand'll stop any bullet."

"Thank you, Mr. Hinkle. There's one other thing, however. Somebody shot at me yesterday from the ceiling, about the middle, where there's about three feet of room between the rafter and the ceiling joist. In the center of the hall, where the rafters peak, there might be over six feet. Is there a way to stop people there?"

Hawkins seemed to think a moment. Then, "You have any ideas?"

"Maybe. I've thought about it. Maybe we could screw four to five-foot-high metal panels to the edges of two by sixes nailed to about every other rafter along the edges of the hall, and pile insulation up against the panels, to make it harder to crawl over the hall. And maybe we could do about the same at the north ends of the rooms, except screw the panels to a scab across a north rafter."

"When should we start?"

"Can you start, and finish today, SueAnn's room first? I think I can be back tomorrow."

"Absolutely we can...we will."

Joe went home to bed. He hoped his later "big guys" would protect SueAnn, as he would have done. His headache had gone down to a dull, heavy feeling by morning, and his first job on Monday morning was to ask another "big guy," John Beels, to sit in the corner by the door. Everything seemed quiet until the fourth period when Sam Ripplinger jumped up from his position in the corner by the door and ran out into the hall. Joe followed and found Sam fighting Tim Klein along the wall, as Ed had done Smithson Reilend. Joe joined the ruckus, and together, he and Sam soon subdued Tim. Mr. Hawkins showed up and insisted they call the police. He looked at Joe, and said, "I know you don't want to call them, but I must do it. After school, Joe went to see Mr. Hinkle. "Did you hear what the police did to Tim Klein?"

"Threw the book at him, I hope."

"No, sir. They turned him loose. They said nobody got hurt, so they had no cause to hold him."

"That's awful, Joe." Hinkle grinned a steely grin. "If I'd known somebody had to get hurt, I'd have made sure it happened-to Tim."

"I could have handled it, Mr. Hinkle. Maybe it could be better to leave it to me next time."

"No, anytime somebody comes into my school with a gun, I'll call the police myself. But not before I make sure the guy with the gun has at least a few broken bones."

It was Joe's turn for the steely grin. "Bravo, Mr. Hinkle."

Nothing happened at school for a while after the Klein problem, but a few weeks later, on the last day of September, SueAnn put her hand over Joe's face at approximately 2 o'clock that morning. As he awoke, he heard her whisper, "Somebody's in here again."

Joe finished waking up quick. He took up his baseball bat, and yelled, "You guys get out of here, NOW!" They left, left the bedroom door open, and went out the open kitchen window. Joe got a glimpse of them as they left, counted three, and recognized both Tim Klein and 'the Erlenmeyer flask.' He felt sure Jake Johns wasn't among them.

Joe closed and locked the kitchen window, checked to see that the boys were OK, went back to bed, and told SueAnn what had happened. They resolved to check all windows before they retired each night and went back to sleep.

The following day, Jake Johns jumped several feet into Joe's room with one jump, during the third hour, Joe's planning period. Jake raised a rifle and hurriedly shot. Joe, though unhit, fell off his desk chair to the floor. Jake took another big jump, back out into the hall, and ran to the north. He dumped his rifle in a trash can by the boys' restroom as he went by. Joe chased Jake but didn't catch him. He came back by the school office and told Mr. Hinkle. Hinkle went out into the hall, saw the rifle barrel, but didn't touch it. He called the police, who sent two officers; they retrieved the rifle and looked for fingerprints. The officers found plenty of fingerprints, but none belonged to a known criminal. Both Mr. Hinkle and Joe tried to tell the police officers about Jake Johns. The officers said they'd include the information in their report; they went away, but Joe could never uncover evidence they'd arrested Jake or had even talked to him.

The following Friday, Joe and SueAnn decided to take the boys and Joseph to the opening Idalou Wildcats football game. Joe called Ed Houser, asked him if he planned to go, learned that he did, and offered to pick him up. Ed accepted, so SueAnn's car went into the high school parking lot full. The game was close, but the Wildcats lost on a touchdown with only a few seconds left in the game. The runner ran right over the little person who replaced Ed Houser They sat, stunned, for a moment or two, during which 'the Round Bottom flask' confronted them. He said, "You don't see it yet, but I have a pistol in my jacket pocket. I plan to shoot you all, then spend the remainder of my glorious life in jail."

Ed didn't rise but swiftly stomped on 'the flask's' foot with his good one. 'The flask' fell through the bleachers, all the way to the turf below. Joseph immediately jumped through as well and landed on 'the flask,' where he stayed. More slowly, Joe went through the bleachers too and stomped on 'the flask has' hand until some fingers were obviously broken, He asked, "Who are you? Why do you want to shoot my family?" The 'flask' didn't answer, but Ed Houser did. He said, "That's Fred Klein, brother of Tim."

SueAnn hunted around until she saw Mr. Hinkle. She asked him to go to the school office and call the police. After she explained, he did. They sent two officers again, they looked at Fred, still underneath Joseph; after Joseph complained mightily to the police about his shoulder, the officers took the guy away in their car.

SueAnn worried about Joseph's shoulder and asked him if he thought he needed an ambulance. He said he didn't. She asked again, and Joseph answered in a cross tone, "No, not unless the police ask about it." SueAnn didn't understand but remained silent.

They took Ed to his parents' home, and SueAnn waited until he opened the front door before she finished the trip to her own home.

When they arrived at their home, the front door hung open, and all lights inside burned brightly. Joe and Joseph went in first, to check, and except for the board over the hole, found nothing. Joe said to SueAnn, "It looks fine. You and the boys can come in now."

"Is anything missing?"

"We didn't look, but nothing I noticed."

SueAnn turned to the boys, and grumbled, "Well, let's go on in. I guess I'll have to look for myself." When inside, she didn't discover anything, and so asked Joe, "Why would somebody break in and not take anything?"

"Maybe to scare us? I have no idea, SueAnn."

"Well, if the purpose is to scare us, it worked, at least for me. Do you think I should make pallets in the kitchen?"

"I'm not that scared, SueAnn. Let's sleep in our own room tonight."

Joe took up the board in front of the front door, locked it, turned off all the lights, and everybody went to bed.

The following Monday, SueAnn felt on edge, all the way through the fifth hour. And sixth hour, a little person she thought she didn't know, appeared at her door, wearing a mask and a baseball cap, holding a big long knife. The other masks had looked professionally made, but this one looked different; it looked like a big red handkerchief popular in the area and covered the person's face. The others had near-elliptical holes for eyes, (and extended down only over the person's nose), but the "ellipses" were pointed on the ends. This mask had only one, round, neatly hemmed eyehole on the right, about an inch and a half across. SueAnn screamed, just as Sean Smith, Joe's sixth hour "big guy in the corner," pushed the little person further into the room; the knife fell on the floor. Joe arrived, crashed into the little person as he put him/her in a bear hug. The person toppled over; Joe instructed Sean, "Put your foot on 'is neck and hold 'im down. He jerked off the mask to discover a woman he didn't think he'd seen before. He spoke, as he withdrew from the bear hug. "I'm sorry, Ma'am. I didn't know you're a woman. Why are you here?" As he asked the last question, his eyes went to the knife on the floor.

The woman didn't answer Joe's question, so he asked people in SueAnn's class, "Anybody know who this is?"

Three people held up hands. Joe called on the nearest. "Susan?"

"Yes, I know. That's Mrs. Terwhiler, wife of the chief of police."

"Thanks, Susan. You've cleared up some things. Will you now go to the office, and ask Mr. Hinkle to come?"

Susan left and soon came back, following Mr. Hinkle. Hinkle took one look, and asked, "What's the meaning of this?"

SueAnn explained, and Joe then asked, "Do you plan to call the police, and if you do, must somebody get hurt?"

"I think I have to call the police, and although I don't intend to hurt anybody physically, I do intend to get some answers."

Joe shook his head. "What answers do you need? Isn't the picture already crystal clear?"

As Joe expected, nothing came of the call to the police. They didn't refuse to show up; they just didn't. Because Joe didn't release the lady, but took her to his classroom and tied her to a desk there, they had a standoff. Joe didn't allow anyone to touch the knife in SueAnn's room, and eventually, about 3:55 pm, Ned Terwhiler, Idalou Police Chief, drug in. He apparently thought a good offense the best defense, because his first words were, "Why do you have my wife tied up?"

Chapter 11

Jake Johns and Other Threats

You have any thoughts about what we should do?" "Perhaps another 'charm offensive?'"

"That's a lot of work, SueAnn. Maybe we can just wait for one of them to make a move."

"Perhaps." SueAnn didn't look convinced, but she apparently felt she could leave it in Joe's hands. They didn't talk about threats anymore, so they adopted Joe's 'sit-back-and-wait' plan by default. But they didn't wait very long. Two days after Junior came home from the hospital, Joe's second hour 'big boy.' Tom Wheeler, pointed at SueAnn. Joe ran for her room and saw a masked person raise a big knotty club over her head.

The club came down before Joe could knock it aside; SueAnn dodged it, although she did suffer a shoulder injury that bothered her for many years. Enraged, Joe dropped a beaker of water to the floor, grabbed the club, wrenched it away from the man, and beat him over the head with it until he crumpled to the floor. The person not only bled from head injuries, but also from his/her left arm, where the broken beaker cut it.

One of SueAnn's students, without being asked, ran out and brought Mr. Hinkle back. He surveyed the scene, grimaced, and said, "Well, plenty of people got hurt. Who's the guy?"

SueAnn said, "I don't know. I'll get the mask off, and maybe I'll recognize him." She pulled the mask off but didn't recognize the person. She asked members of her class to help, but no one had a clue, She turned to Mr. Hinkle, and admitted, "I guess we don't know."

Hinkle responded, "Tommy, will you run down to the office and ask June to call the police? I'll stay here until they come."

A couple of police officers soon showed up, looked at the man's driver's license, and identified him as Peter F. Jones of Houston. No one present had heard about him, but Joe commented, "Well, there's another one we didn't know about. I wonder how much more like that are out there?"

Hinkle grimaced again. "We'll never know until the attacks end." Joe noted the 'we' in Hinkle's statement and felt Mr. Hinkle'd been drawn into the fight, on his side.

The police officers took Jones away. Joe knew, however, Jake Johns and possibly others, remained. SueAnn decided to remain at school and to try to ignore her shoulder wound.

Everything remained quiet for a couple of days. Joe used the time to stretch a trip cord across the hall to the bedrooms and to attach it to the same bell that rang when someone fell into the hole he dug by the door. After a couple more days, he and SueAnn heard a heavy thud, then the bell at about two ten am. Joe ran out of the bedroom, brandishing his ball bat, and saw two people go out the kitchen window. He ran to look and thought he recognized Jake Johns, plus a woman. About midway through the third hour, on Tuesday, December 4, Joe heard SueAnn scream. He didn't have a big boy in the corner because he had no class during that hour, so he ran to SueAnn's room alone. He saw a masked person, maybe a woman, holding what looked like a pointed paring knife, aimed at SueAnn's neck, with one ofSueAnn's students creeping up behind the person. Joe startled her but stopped. The student grabbed her arm, wrestled the knife away, and twisted her arm behind her back until she yelped. One of the students in the class ran to get Mr. Hinkle, who arrived within about a minute. He jerked off the mask and found a woman underneath. Joe asked Mr. Hinkle, "Who is she?"

Hinkle answered, "Your guess is as good as mine. Do you know?" When Joe shook his head, Hinkle asked people in the class. No one knew. Mr. Hinkle asked the boy holding the lady's arm to continue, then asked both Joe and SueAnn to follow him to the office. He asked June to find a teacher to take SueAnn's class and to call the police.

He took Joe and SueAnn into his private office, and said, "My responsibility here is to the students and the school. Although I think you're both good teachers, and although I value the friendship of both of you, I won't extend your contract at the end of the year unless you get this attack business over before then. Neither of you has tenure, but even if you did, no court in the state would expect me to tolerate all the disruptions you two have been party to." Mr. Hinkle paused, and Joe started to speak, but Mr. Hinkle continued. "Until the end of the year, I plan to ask the local police department to station an officer in each of your rooms. That will protect you, but will also cost the school district."

Joe responded, "Even with the new chief I don't trust the local police. Could you post a Texas Ranger in our rooms instead?"

"Out of the question. It would cost more." "How about if we paid the difference?"

"I'll check with the school board. Let's go find out who the unidentified woman is."

They went back to SueAnn's room, and Mr. Hinkle asked, "Who is she?" "We don't know, Sir. She has no identification on her, and she won't tell us."

The woman opened her mouth. "Do you think I look so stupid as to carry identification, or to tell you?"

An officer said, "We'll take you down to our interrogation room at the station, and we'll get it out of you."

Joe spoke to Mr. Hinkle. "Could we send her directly to Austin? I'll be happier if the Texas Rangers ask her."

"I'll ask June to call them on the telephone, and check."

The Rangers sent a person to take the woman to their headquarters at Austin. Early the next morning, a Ranger called Mr. Hinkle's office on the telephone. He said, "The lady is Madge Felkengritch of Tyler. She said you've already killed or jailed most of their people in the Idalou-Lubbock area, so she went. It's my personal opinion that not many people will travel as far as Madge did so that you may have already about ended the threat. However, I recommend you quickly institute a metal check on every person entering the building and have all deliveries and mail sent to your office, to be opened there, in case anyone wants to smuggle in a weapon. Joe Alley asked if we'll put a guard in his room and in Mrs. Alley's room until the end of the school year, and of course, the answer is yes, at no charge, but only until the end of the school year, We'll also put a couple of guards at his home, at the same non-cost." Mr. Hinkle followed the recommendation about metal detectors and packages.

The guards in the rooms were effective. No more attacks occurred there for a while, or at the Alley home; one guard slept in Joseph's room, with his back against the inward-opening door, and another similarly slept in the boys' room.

Even so, SueAnn whispered to Joe, during a mid-January night in their room, that she thought someone might be in their room. Joe reached for a bed-light switch, to prove otherwise; he had a lot of confidence in the holes in front of the doors, and in the trip-string, he'd put in. But when the light came on, he saw Jake Johns hover over SueAnn, with a long knife in his hand. Joe reached for his bat, gave a mighty swing, and yelled, "Get outta here!" Jake, however, partly deflected the swing, the bat touched SueAnn on her chest instead of smashing Jake's skull as Joe intended.

His yell did at least wake Jack, the Texas Ranger next door in Joseph's room, who showed up in time to trip over the string as Jake disappeared out the window. After a short conversation, Jack and Joe went back to bed, but Joe didn't sleep much during the remainder of the night.

Jack suggested to Joe and SueAnn the next morning at breakfast that they keep the kitchen window closed and locked at night. SueAnn said they did, but Joe felt the Ranger wasn't sure of that; Joe suggested Jack go over everything every night, and change it as he saw fit. Jack seemed happy, and Joe thought he'd never find anything to change, as he didn't, even though Jake somehow gained entry two more times before the new year.

That will protect you, but will also cost the school district."

Joe responded, "Even with the new chief I don't trust the local police. Could you post a Texas Ranger in our rooms instead?"

"Out of the question. It would cost more." "How about if we paid the difference?"

"I'll check with the school board. Let's go find out who the unidentified woman is." They went back to SueAnn's room, and Mr. Hinkle asked, "Who is she?"

"We don't know, Sir. She has no identification on her, and she won't tell us."

The woman opened her mouth. "Do you think I look so stupid as to carry identification, or to tell you?"

An officer said, "We'll take you down to our interrogation room at the station, and we'll get it out of you."

Joe spoke to Mr. Hinkle. "Could we send her directly to Austin? I'll be happier if the Texas Rangers ask her."

"I'll ask June to call them on the telephone, and check."

The Rangers sent a person to take the woman to their headquarters at Austin. Early the next morning, a Ranger called Mr. Hinkle's office on the telephone. He said, "The lady is Madge Felkengritch of Tyler. She said you've already killed or jailed most of their people in the Idalou-Lubbock area, and that's why she went there. It's my personal opinion that not many people will travel as far as Madge did so that you may have already about ended the threat. However, I recommend you quickly institute a metal check on every person entering the school building and have all deliveries and mail sent to your office, to be opened there, in case anyone wants to smuggle in a weapon. Joe Alley asked if we'll put a guard in his room and in Mrs. Alley's room until the end of the school year, and of course, the answer is yes, at no charge, but only until the end of the school year. We'll also put a couple of guards at his home, at the same non-cost." Mr. Hinkle followed the recommendation about metal detectors and packages.

The guards in the rooms were effective. No more attacks occurred there for a while, or at the Alley home; one guard slept in Joseph's room, with his back against the inward-opening door, and another similarly slept in the boys' room.

Even so, SueAnn whispered to Joe, during a mid-January night in their room, that she thought someone might be in their room. Joe reached for a bed-light switch, to prove otherwise; he had a lot of confidence in the holes in front of the doors, and in the trip-string, he'd put in. But when the light came on, he saw Jake Johns hover over SueAnn, with a long knife in his hand. Joe reached for his bat, gave a mighty swing, and yelled, "Get outta here!" Jake, however, partly deflected the swing, the bat touched SueAnn on her chest instead of smashing Jake's skull as Joe intended.

His yell did at least wake Jack, the Texas Ranger next door in Joseph's room, who showed up in time to hook his foot under the string and watch as Jake disappeared out the window. After a short conversation, Jack and Joe went back to bed, but Joe didn't sleep much during the remainder of the night.

Joe looked gratefully at Bob. "This might be the last of them. The end of the school year will come soon, and we'll see."

Bob rejoined, "I'm only here until the end of the school year. The same goes for Jack and Steve in your house, and for Sam, who should be here right now. I think he's in Austin this week; he picked a terrible week to be gone!"

Joe asked, "What would a security guard cost for our house, at night only." "Forty to fifty an hour. I recommend it."

"SueAnn and I'll talk about it."

That evening after school, as they drove home, Joe commented, "There's no way we can afford forty bucks an hour, even if we both can keep our jobs. We'll just have to rely on Dad, as we did before."

"I agree, Joe. We'd only last about a week, then we'd have to go into our savings, and that wouldn't last forever, either."

"I'm not that scared, SueAnn. Let's sleep in our own room tonight." Joe took up the board in front of the front door, locked it, turned off all the lights, and everybody went to bed.

The following Monday, SueAnn felt on edge, all the way through the fifth hour. And sixth hour, a little person she thought she didn't know, appeared at her door, wearing a mask and a baseball cap, holding a big long knife. The other masks had looked professionally made, but this one looked different; it looked like a big red handkerchief popular in the area and covered the person's face. The others had near-elliptical holes for eyes, (and extended down only over the person's nose), but the "ellipses" were pointed on the ends. This mask had only one, round, neatly hemmed eyehole on the right, about an inch and a half across. SueAnn screamed, just as Sean Smith, Joe's sixth hour "big guy in the corner," pushed the little person further into the room; the knife fell on the floor.

Joe arrived, crashed into the little person as he put him/her a bear hug. The person toppled over; Joe instructed Sean, "Put your foot on 'is neck and hold em' down. He jerked off the mask to discover a woman he didn't think he'd seen before. He spoke, as he withdrew from the bear hug. "I'm sorry, Ma'am. I didn't know you're a woman. Why are you here?" As he asked the last question, his eyes went to the knife on the floor.

The woman didn't answer Joe's question, so he asked people in SueAnn's class, "Anybody know who this is?"

Three people held up hands. Joe called on the nearest. "Susan?"

"Yes, I know. That's Mrs. Terwhiler, wife of the cl1ief of police."

"Thanks, Susan. You've cleared up some things. Will you now go to the office, and ask Mr. Hinkle to come?"

Susan left and soon came back, following Mr. Hinkle. Hinkle took one look, and asked, "What's the meaning of this?"

SueAnn explained, and Joe then asked, "Do you plan to call the police, and if you do, must somebody get hurt?"

"I think I have to call the police, and although I don't intend to hurt anybody physically, I do intend to get some answers."

Joe shook his head. "What answers do you need? Isn't the picture already crystal clear?"

As Joe expected, nothing came of the call to the police. They didn't refuse to show up; they just didn't. Because Joe didn't release the lady, but took her to his classroom and tied her to a desk there, they had a standoff. Joe didn't allow anyone to touch the knife in SueAnn's room, and eventually, about 3:55 pm, Ned Terwhiler, Idalou Police Chief, drug in. He apparently thought a good offense the best defense, because his first words were, "Why do you have my wife tied up?"

Joe responded, 'Maybe you should tell me, Sir."

The Chief sputtered, "How could I do that, Sonny Boy?" He untied his wife and strode to the door with her.

"If you don't know, then I suggest you ask her."

As the chief and his wife went out the door, and just before he bumped into Mr. Hinkle, he said over his shoulder, "You're in big trouble, Sonny Boy."

Mr. Hinkle suggested the Terwhilers go into his office to talk, but Joe eventually saw Mr. and Mrs. Terwhiler, pass his room, go down the stair, and out the door. He stormed down to Mr. Hinkle's office, but Mr. Hinkle stopped him with a raised hand. "I talked turkey to the Chief, and he claimed he'd lock his wife in a cell overnight, and find a lawyer for her tomorrow."

"Well, I guess overnight's better than not at all."

Mr. Hinkle smiled. "Relax, Joe. I've made this my fight, and I intend to win." "Maybe there's nothing I can do, so good luck, Sir."

The Idalou City Council met the following week and fired Chief Terwhiler. His wife remained in jail until she raised $100,000 bail, eventually lost in court, and was sentenced to four years at Roach State Prison.

Chapter 12

The Roundbottom Flask

A few days later, on a Tuesday, November six, very early, a few minutes after one am, Joe "felt" a presence in his bedroom. He cautiously opened his eyes, but because of darkness, saw nothing. He felt for his baseball bat, grabbed it, and waited for his eyes to adjust. He eventually saw three people-he recognized two; the 'round bottom flask' and Jake Johns. Although he didn't want to wake or to scare SueAnn, he yelled, "Get out!"

The three fled. They put the board over the hole by the front door, opened it, and ran out. Joe removed the board, closed and locked the door, and returned to bed. After a short explanation to SueAnn, he went back to sleep.

Early in November, the Idalou school board canceled school on a Thursday and Friday, in favor of a teacher's meeting in Austin. Joe decided to skip the Thursday sessions and to try to see what he could learn about the other flask. He looked up Ace Best in the phone book, and learned his residence address, and that his real name is Otto, which he already knew. He warned Joseph to be careful about the boys and rented a blue over white Chevrolet Chevelle (not a red Ford Falcon) for SueAnn to drive to Austin; he thought people might not recognize the car, and that SueAnn could safely drive it to Austin. Thursday morning, he parked his F-150 about three blocks away from Best's house at four a.m and settled down to wait. Eventually, at seven forty am, a green, late model Buick backed out of Best's garage. It headed toward downtown Lubbock, and Joe followed, at a discreet distance. The Buick stopped at a car dealership on J Street, and Best went inside. Joe knew it was Best because he could never forget his profile! He parked, again about three blocks away, on J Street. At nearly noon, Ace came back outside, and drove his Buick northwest, out the Clovis road, toward Shallowater. Joe followed. Ace stopped in front of a large pink warehouse, at least fifty ft by a hundred feet. Another warehouse, painted blue, sat near the pink one, a few feet to the right of it. Best entered a door at the left front end of the pink warehouse and came back out about ten minutes later. Joe noted the two warehouses were mirror images, except for color. Best drove away, but Joe didn't follow. After Best had been gone a few minutes, Joe walked to the same door Best had used, and opened it as if he owned it. He looked around and didn't see anyone. He saw only a few overstuffed chairs and a coffeepot. He didn't see anything he thought interesting. He walked a few feet inside, and then he saw a man, wearing a holster with a huge pistol in it. The man didn't try to shoot Joe, but said,

"You'd best get out of this building, Bud." Joe got out as fast as he could, walked to his F-150, and drove a few blocks until he couldn't see the warehouse any longer. After a while, he drove farther, and parked in front of a cafe, went inside, and ordered breakfast. After he finished breakfast, he ordered lunch, and ate that! He went back outside, drove to a bookstore, and read a book there. Eventually, it got dark, and he went back to the warehouse area. A streetlight stood in front of the two warehouses, but sort of between, so it illuminated the fronts, the right side of the pink one and the left side of the blue one. Joe went down the dark (right) side of the blue one; he noticed the three windows were each covered by thick curtains, and no door existed on the right side. He went around the corner to the back and found two large dogs back there. They were tied with heavy chains, but they barked and snarled so much, Joe decided to turn around and go back. He waited in the dark a few moments before he went into the lighted area in front, but when he did, nothing happened.

He cautiously went down the left side of the blue building and saw a door near the back. When he reached the door, he tried it, and it opened. He went inside, leaving the door open; he took a couple of steps, looked around, saw a bunch of crosses, some statues of men on horses, and even saw a scarecrow, painted black, hang from a ceiling joist. He heard the door latch and whirled around. The same guy he'd encountered in the pink building stood just behind him. Joe had noticed the guy looked older, and thought he could easily outrun him, but he knew he couldn't outrun the big pistol. He ran anyway, and the guy didn't pull out the pistol. Joe ran for the door in front but found it locked. His pursuer said, "There's no need to run to the back door. I locked it when I came in." Joe jumped through some curtained glass in the front door, and rolled up at the feet of Ace Best, holding a leash with a snarling dog at the other end! Considering Ace's physique, Joe felt confident he could outrun him, but he knew he had no chance with the dog. He jumped up and ran anyway; Ace held onto the leash, but Joe felt teeth graze the back of his thigh as he ran. He ran all the way to his truck, jumped in, shut the door, fumbled for his key, and sped away. Ace, perhaps pulled by the dog, slammed into the truck door just as Joe put the truck in gear; the truck dragged him a few feet, but he soon fell away. Joe didn't slow down, however, until he made it home. When there, he told his dad about the big pistol and estimated the barrel must be at least 1 ½ inches across. Joseph expressed doubt!

Joe didn't get to stay long at his home because he wanted to go back into Lubbock and catch a red-eye bus to Austin. The bus required eleven hours for the trip, through San Angelo. Joe began the trip at five after ten at night, and arrived at Austin a few minutes early, at about nine am. He hurried to a meeting of chemistry teachers, and ultimately, shortly after four pm, met SueAnn at a restaurant they'd earlier agreed on. After their evening meal, they started home. They went through San Angelo, then to Snyder, and a little beyond, when Joe looked in the rear-view mirror, then looked again. He said, "Headlights are coming up on us fast."

SueAnn didn't seem much concerned, but suggested, "Perhaps you can go just a little faster."

"They're really coming on. We'll see what a Chevelle can do." Joe floored the Chevelle, and it crept up to ninety-eight, and then up to slightly over one hundred miles per hour. "Those lights are still gaining, and the Chevelle is flat out." Suddenly they felt a crash. Joe yelled, "They rear-ended us, SueAnn." SueAnn put her hand over her mouth; the jolt enabled the Caprice to go a few more mph faster, but they soon felt another crash, and SueAnn gave a short scream. "I think I'll put the brakes on, nice and easy, when they rear-end us again."

When the third crash happened, Joe carefully applied a small amount of brake and slowed both vehicles a bit, but the pursuer dropped back, and rear-ended the Chevelle again, harder, because of the smaller Chevelle speed. Joe repeated his slow-down operation, the pursuing lights dropped back, and Joe slowed even more, down to around eighty-five mph. The pursuing lights came alongside the Chevelle and tried to force it off the road. Joe yelled at SueAnn again. "That's a green Buick. It might belong to Roundbottom." The Buick dropped back again, and Joe quickly summarized his actions of the day before. "Maybe I got his attention! Maybe he's mad at me! I'm pretty sure that's Ace Best at the wheel."

After a few more 'faceoff' attempts, they came to a small town called Justiceburg. Joe slowed to the speed limit as he entered the town and stopped at a gas station there. The green Buick went on past the station. Joe said to the attendant, "fill 'er up" and went inside to use the telephone. SueAnn followed him. He called the car rental agency, and explained, sort of, but didn't mention Ace Best. He also said he'd parked at a gas station in Justiceburg. The person at the car rental place asked if he could stay for at least four hours. Joe responded, "This is Saturday morning, I can stay for at least ten times that long if the green Buick doesn't show up again."

"Great. Three guys'll be out in about four hours with a completely different vehicle for you. They'll be armed, and will bring the Chevelle back here." Joe explained to SueAnn, and they settled down on bar stools to wait.

After about four hours and ten minutes, three men came through the door, and one pointed to a ton GMC with a two-wheel trailer outside the station. He said, "That's your new rig. Don't go faster than forty mph, because the trailer'll whip. And you won't see the plates, but we have bullet-proof plates behind the driver and passenger positions.

Joe rubbed sleepy eyes and said, "We're ready." They went out to the GMC, started it, and started again for Idalou. The Chevelle passed them, but headlights from behind soon crashed into them. Joe slowed, and said to SueAnn, "Maybe I should stop and take a tire tool to that ornery Best.

"Oh no, Joe. He might have a gun, and might shoot you."

"I'll try something else then." He floored the GMC until he had it to about fifty mph. The trailer whipped, the lights rear-ended it and swerved almost into the side-ditch. 'We might get the guy if he pulls a stunt like that again." Joe continued at about fifty mph, but the lights, (attached to a green Buick!) came alongside and tried to force the GMC off the road. Joe jerked the wheel of the GMC hard left, and almost forced the Buick off.

"He had more weight than a Chevelle, but this outfit weighs than he does. He probably won't try that again." Joe slowed to about twenty mph, however, in an effort to lure the Buick beside. Instead, he heard a bullet splat behind him somewhere, it caused SueAnn to put her hand on her mouth, but she didn't say anything. "I think I'll just forget about Ace, and drive along at forty mph. I don't think there's anything he can do." SueAnn looked even more worried than before, if that were possible, but said nothing.

They were home about ten am Saturday morning. Joe and SueAnn collapsed into bed and didn't awaken until the wee hours of Sunday. All the Alleys went to church on Sunday, and came home, but about midafternoon, while the boys should have been napping Joseph burst into the living room and all but yelled, "Roundbottom has kidnapped Junior."

Both Joe and SueAnn turned white, questioning faces toward Joseph. He explained, "I intended to watch them, but I must have dozed a bit. I became aware Roundbottom had climbed down a short stepladder into the room from the window. He grabbed Junior by one foot and one arm and literally threw him out the window. I heard junior hit the lawn, and then cry, as Roundbottom quickly climbed his inside ladder, I watched him step onto an outside ladder against the house, then grab Junior again, and take him up a ladder against the south fence, and again literally throw him from the top of the ladder into the alley. I couldn't hear the impact that time, but I heard Junior's louder cry. Both SueAnn and Joe sat motionless, trying to take it all in for a moment.

Joe jumped toward the front door as he reached into his pocket for his truck keys. He said, "I'll be gone a while," started his truck, backed out into the street headed south, and careened into the alley. He caught a glimpse of a green Buick turn right off the alley up ahead. Joe followed.

He decided before his first turn; he'd turn right again when he came to a street. His guess (right) turned out to be correct, and the green Buick, more battered now, turned left up ahead. Joe followed again and decided he'd turn left when he came to the next street. Either he guessed wrong, or Ace had proven too fast because he didn't see a green Buick after his turn. Joe couldn't admit failure yet, so he went to Lubbock, drove around the loop a couple of times, but didn't see Ace. He started a third time around but turned off to go past the warehouses.

Joe didn't, quite properly, claim a favorite between his two boys, but Junior had always been a trace taller, a trace heavier, and had always dominated in wrestling and other sibling rivalries, to the extent that Robby didn't even challenge him anymore.

He drove by the warehouses and saw no green Buick there. He went to Ace's home, looked in the garage window, and saw no vehicle. So finally, and dejectedly, he headed home.

When Joe came through his front door, before he was even off the board over the hole, SueAnn talked. "We got a ransom call from 'round bottom! He wants a million dollars in unmarked bills, with no police."

Joe didn't brighten. "Where we gonna get a million dollars?" SueAnn almost gushed. "Joseph says he'll get it for us!"

Joe looked even glummer. "We can't take Dad's money, SueAnn."

Joseph said, "I can borrow most of it against my place in Post. And Claude can borrow the rest of it against his ranch-it's almost paid for. It's the least I can do. It was my job to keep the boys safe, and I didn't.

Claude doesn't want to call his banker on Sunday, but I already called mine, at home. And I recommend we call Junior's Sunday School teacher at the church and get a temporary loan just for today."

Joe continued his glum look but possibly lightened it just a bit. He said, "I'll pay you back, Dad, regardless how long it takes. I might have to change jobs, but I'll pay you back. Did the guy give a callback number?"

SueAnn said, "It's all my fault. Junior deserved a better childhood than this, and he'd have had it if people didn't hate me! It's not Junior's fault at all.

Joe looked thoughtful. "Did you say no police? I don't want to involve local guys, but I bet the Texas Rangers would actually help. Did the caller establish a meeting time or place?"

"He did, and he specified I should bring the money." SueAnn looked determined.

Joe looked equally determined. "Not chance. I'll take the money."

"But Joe, what if it means the guy doesn't give Junior back?"

"You think you're less valuable than Junior?"

Joseph talked a bit about maybe he should take the money, but Joe nixed that idea too

Joe asked, "So when and where?"

SueAnn looked at her watch, and said "Four pm. He said at the pink warehouse. I don't know where that is."

Joe looked at his, and said, "It's almost three now. You think the Texas Rangers will go along with anything that soon? I know exactly where the pink warehouse is."

SueAnn stood, and answered, "There' only one way to find out. I'll call them." She almost ran to the kitchen, looked in the phone book, and called.

The dispatcher she talked with said, "How can we help you?" She explained. The dispatcher said, "We got two officers in Lubbock at a meeting, to be over about now. Who's going to get the boy?"

"My husband?"

"Put 'em on."

Joe spoke into the telephone. "Hello"

The dispatcher immediately told him, "Just go on out to the warehouse at four. We know where it is, and will be there ahead of you, but you won't see us. We want to know who kidnapped your son, and—"

"I know who did it. His name is—"

"It don't matter, Mr. . . ."

"Alley. Joe Alley."

"It don't matter, Mr. Alley. We want to see ourselves. Again, you won't see us, and neither will the perp. But we'll be there."

"Will you make me wear a . . . wire, or whatever you call it?"

"Naw, my guys'll just look and listen."

Joe went, and arrived at almost exactly four pm. He planned to see the front door of the pink warehouse and walked a few steps inside. He saw Ace sitting in a chair near the middle of the building, with a tight hold on Junior.

A he walked toward the chair, Ace asked, "You bring the money?"

Joe answered, "Ye, and you can have it after you let Junior loose."

"How about we do it at the same time? That is, you grab the kid at the same time you give me the money."

Joe didn't answer, but he planned to have a very strong hold on both Junior and the money, and to see Ace loosen his grip on Junior before he released the money. But when he stopped in front of Ace's chair, he almost threw the money at him, and grabbed at Junior. Ace held on to Junior, however, but a Texas Ranger suddenly stood behind his chair, put a pistol to the back of Ace's head, and ordered, "Give back the money, and the boy."

Chapter 13

The New House

"Do you suppose the tunnel is big enough Max Rafael could have gotten his pickup through it."

"I measured it. It's eight feet high, nine feet wide, and so yes, any pickup should go through there."

"Great, Dad. That explains how Max did it."

Joe used the telephone in the school office Tuesday, during the third period, his off time, to ask the City to dump gravel or dirt into the alley end of the hole. That night, he also put pieces of iron rebar into some spaces above the plate and below the rim so that the top couldn't be raised.

Joe and SueAnn talked about the design of a new house, and agreed on most things, except SueAnn wanted bars on the windows, a deadbolt on the front and back doors, plus an interior 2 x 6 across each door, like on a seldom-used barn door. Joe didn't.

"That will be ugly, SueAnn, especially the 2 x 6's."

"We only need the 2 x 6's while we sleep; the bars will be outside, and we can cover them with curtains."

"I still don't like it."

"Not even the deadbolts?"

"That part's all right, I guess, but I don't see that it's needed."

"It's not, Joe, when you're here to protect me, but you're not here all the time."

Joe succumbed to the flattery and agreed to it all. So they planned a house similar to the old one, except for the bars and 2 x 6's downstairs, plus a couple more changes; it had, a kitchen, living room, laundry room, and furnace room on the first floor, with a stair leading out of the kitchen, which sat on the north of the first floor, up to the east, to a landing. From the landing, people could walk east to the 'master bedroom,' or down a hall south, past the guest rooms, and on to the boys' room. The change amounted to making the house a foot longer and wider, all bedrooms upstairs slightly smaller, and adding a second guest room. One of the guest rooms was designated Joseph's room and sat next to the boys' room. One or the extra wrinkles Joe had gotten from his tour with Clifford Wyman was a laundry chute, set in a bump-out in the hall, (visible from the outside of the house) just across the hall from the master bedroom; the other had to do with the fireplace, and a wider mantle than the old house had had. They planned to set the house on a concrete slab. Once they agreed on the design, Joe could hardly wait for school to end so he could begin to build. Before school ended, Joe went to the Idalou City hall to apply for a building permit. A person called a "Codes Officer," started to give Joe a hard time, but Joe had already resolved to hold his temper, and to get along with City hall if at all possible. The "codes officer" first objected to the laundry chute. He claimed the chute would be act as a chimney for a fire and said Joe must put a "fire block" somewhere in it, to prevent the chimney effect. Joe understood that, and immediately decided to install two fire blocks-one at the bottom, over a countertop on a cabinet adjacent to the washer, and another at the top, at the right height for Junior and

Robby to sit on it. But then, the "codes officer" then criticized Joe's plan for a stairway. Joe planned it twenty-nine inches wide, like the one in his old house, but the "codes officer" wanted it to be thirty-six inches wide.

Joe almost blew up. He said, "The stairway in my old house was twenty-nine, and it worked just fine. If I make it thirty-six, it'll take up too much space."

"Did you say your father lives with you? How old is he?"

Joe thought the "code officer's" question over the bounds of decency, so he shrugged, and answered, "I'm not sure. How old are you?"

They argued much over Joseph's age, and Joe never understood a reason why his age mattered to the "codes officer," but he finally stated Joseph's age as "somewhere between fifty-five and sixty-five." The "codes officer" seemed satisfied, but still required Joe to make the stairs thirty-six inches wide, with a handrail up one side. Joe decided that was the best he could do, so he agreed; the "codes officer signed off on the plan, and Joe left the City Hall.

School ended May 20, and Joe began digging for the foundation the next day. By Saturday evening, he'd dug it all, sixteen inches deep, had leveled up the interior, and was ready to have trucks spread gravel on places he intended to put concrete. He and SueAnn came back out near dark on Saturday and admired his work. A truck arrived on Monday, and the driver didn't want to unload. He claimed he'd push the loose dirt Joe had piled up outside the foundation, back into the ditch. Joe argued, "Do it, then, and I'll clean it out again."

The driver asked, "How many houses you built, Son?"

Although a truthful answer would have to be none, Joe answered, "Enough, Pops."

"You move the loose dirt out a couple of feet, then call me."

"I don't plan to move it an inch. You drive in there, and unload." "Bye, Son."

Joe swallowed hard. He said, "Just unload it outside the foundation area, and I'll shove it in."

"You sure?" I'm sure."

"Whatever you want, Son." The driver dumped an entire load of gravel between the street and the house site.

"Thanks, Pops."

Joe labored all day Monday and Tuesday, but ended with a smooth, well-distributed gravel layer. He next installed boards to hold concrete for the foundation in place. He called for a ready-mix truck the next day. He had the same problem with the ready-mix truck driver he'd had earlier! The driver said, "I ain't got no pump. I can't back across your ditches to the back, without messing up your boards."

"How long will it take you to go back and get a pump to bring?" "Listen, Bud, I ain't got all day. I'll fill the ditches in front, and dump the rest of my load anywhere on your lot you want it. But I gotta get unloaded."

"Can you just unload enough to fill the front foundation, then take the rest of the concrete to your next job, and maybe come back someday when you can back over the front foundation?"

"Listen, Bud. You ordered what you ordered. I can't take it back."
"Well, fill the front foundation then, and dump the remainder anywhere you like." The driver did and dumped the rest of the concrete out by the street. Joe moved as much as he could before it got too stiff, into the nearest end foundation.

The next day, he ordered the concrete he still needed from another supplier and specified a pump. The guy showed up on Friday. Saturday, Joe removed all the temporary forms he'd made, and Monday, called the second concrete company to bring concrete for the floor. He didn't think he'd need a pump, and when he explained the front had been poured on Wednesday, the concrete company agreed he wouldn't need a pump if he waited until the front concrete was a week old. The receptionist said the truck could just back over the front if it had been in place a week. So, Joe waited a day. He did nothing except put down some piping for water in, and for sewage out. The truck came on Wednesday morning, and, with Joseph's and SueAnn's help, he installed and smoothed the slab he intended the house to sit on.

Thursday, he began the east exterior wall, but had only laid out the lumber when a person he didn't know showed up and asked, "Building a better one?"

"That's my plan. Who are you?"

"Somebody you don't know, but I'm gonna kill you." The guy pulled a pistol and pointed it at Joe.

Joe's hand instinctively went to his hammer in the hammer loop of his overalls. His mind raced. "You are forgetting about the sniper on the roof of the house next door?" He jerked his head barely south, and the guy looked, for only a fraction of a second, but long enough. Joe pulled his hammer from the loop and threw it at the guy's pistol. He didn't hit the pistol, or even the right arm holding it, but he did hit the other arm. The man screamed, dropped his pistol, and then tried to pick it up. Joe, however, slammed a 2 x 4 he'd picked up, down on the guy's right hand and caused him to scream again, then turn and run. Joe yelled, "You better run, you slimy snake," but then he ran to his rented home. He could have asked one of Beth's hired 'guards' to watch, but instead, he asked Joseph. He helped Joseph put a ladder up the back side of Roy Johnson's now vacant home, borrowed Art Cline's squirrel gun, and Joseph took a position on the former Roy's roof. Soon after, Joe went to the base of the house, and asked Joseph not to point the gun in his direction unless someone tried to kill him!

Joe returned to his wall work, and raised the east wall, but had only started on the south one when the guy who'd accosted him earlier, returned. The man said, "You won't escape this time. I got you this time." Joe answered, "You're forgetting again about the sniper," as he inclined his head slightly north.

"That trick worked once, but it won't work again." The man pulled the pistol once again from a holster and raised it. Just then, a squirrel gun blast hit him in the back of the head. The gun, only a .410, didn't kill the man but did take him to his knees. Joe rushed him, but the man recovered quickly, turned, and ran. Joe only got a piece of shirt, plus the pistol the man left behind as he ran.

Joe yelled at Joseph, "Excellent work, Dad." He went closer, to talk more quietly to Joseph. His dad agreed to stay indefinitely, but when the man didn't come back that week or the next, Joe told his dad he might as well return the squirrel gun and go back to watching the boys.

The unknown assailant didn't return until Joe had all the walls up and worked at installing gable trusses for the roof. He showed up and caught Joe up on top. He pointed his pistol again, but Joe threw his hammer at the guy and hit the guy on the left wrist-not the one he held the gun with, but the man dropped the gun anyway. Joe jumped all the way to the concrete floor, fell to his knees, got up, picked up a board with a bad-looking nail in the end, and chased the guy away. After that happened, he put up a piece of sheet rock for Joseph to hide behind, then went directly home, and asked Joseph to borrow the squirrel gun again.

After lunch, he and Joseph went back to the building site, and Joseph finished the trusses without further incident, but at roughly midnight that night, Joe awakened with an uneasy feeling. He got out of bed, went to the front room, and saw no one. But he did see the beginning of his new house, on fire! He called the fire department and returned to bed.

SueAnn asked, "What was that all about?"

Joe mumbled a non-answer, and fell asleep, but had to explain in more detail the next morning.

SueAnn asked, "What do you plan to do about it?"

"Nothing. Maybe I'll sleep a lot this summer."

SueAnn looked incensed. "Sleep!? Somebody burns your work, and you plan to sleep?"

Joseph had opened his mouth, but closed it, and appeared to try to be invisible. SueAnn continued. "You need to get yourself out there, take Joseph for protection, and start today to rebuild!

A flash of anger showed in Joe's eyes. "What's the use, SueAnn? Nothing I do goes unchallenged. Nothing works."

"So, the way to meet a challenge is head-on. If you don't go, Joseph and I will, right Joseph?"

A Joseph appeared to try even harder to be invisible., but Joe rescued him. "No, SueAnn, you mustn't go. I'll go. I won't like it, but I'll go."

Both SueAnn and Joseph seemed to relax a bit. Joe continued, "I looked out this morning, and could see nothing worth trying to save. The concrete might be all right, though."

Joe looked at his dad and continued further. If I have a pile of lumber unloaded on the site, for you to hide behind, will you borrow the squirrel gun again, and go also?"

"You know I want to help in any way I can, Son."

Joe ordered a load of lumber, to be delivered, the following week. In the meantime, he waited and became more interested as he did. Also, while he waited, he took two gasoline cans he found to local gas stations. One attendant remembered selling the gasoline. In response to Joe's questions, he described the buyer as male, well dressed, driving a car with an out-of-state license, possibly California. Joe couldn't think who that might be, so when the lumber arrived, he and Joseph went to the site, and Joe spent much of the day tearing down what he'd already built. No one came to interfere, however. He spent almost a week replacing the burned walls, but when he had two adjacent walls up, he made another place for Joseph to sit, out of sight of the road out front. This time, he used plywood sheathing to make his 'Joseph-hiding-place.' It was good he did, because a long-wet spell came along during the follow-ing week, and if he'd used sheetrock as before, it would have dissolved.

After Joe put up all the walls and prepared to sheath, he began to take down the stack of the plywood sheathing for Joseph to hide behind. He didn't notice when a white car with out-of-state license plates drove past. As the car went by, two rifles poked out the windows, and each fired. The bullets narrowly missed both Joe and his father.' Joe suggested, "Maybe we ought to call it a day,"

Joseph replied, "I'm for that."

They both went back to Beth's house.

Sue Ann waited for them there. She said, "I saw the car and heard the shots. I planned to wait about another minute, then to come and check on you."

Joe asked, "Did you get a license number?"

"N"

"No."

"How about a make of car?"

"No; it was white."

'That's all we can say, too.

The next day Joseph and Joe returned to the building site. Joseph took care to stay behind the pile of sheathing and to keep the squirrel gun close, but nothing happened that day, a Tuesday.

They finished the walls and the roof by Wednesday of the following week still without incident and felt safer inside after Wednesday. After about another month they moved into their new house on Saturday and Monday before school began.

Nothing bad had happened after the white car problem the day Helen ran away from home, so Joe mentioned Helen as a possible person behind all the trouble to the Texas. They came to Joe during the third week of school and asked if they'd had any more problems.

Joe said "No."

The spokesman for the Rangers said, "We think the ringleader of the bunch has been Helen, and we know where she is."

"Where?"

"Los Angeles, California. We can get her extradited to stand trial here if you want us to."

"Let me talk to SueAnn."

Joe and SueAnn talked. Joe said to the Ranger, "It's been so quiet lately, we don't want to upset the applecart. We think we'll pass on the extradition."

Chapter 14

The Erlenmeyer Flask

With Helen gone, nothing happened for a few months. But then, the Erlenmeyer Flask showed up in SueAnn's room. During Joe's free period, he'd sat at a student desk near the back of the chemistry room for a while, but after about a month of no attacks, he'd gone back to his desk at the front. One Wednesday, however, he heard screams from SueAnn's room during his free period. He ran into SueAnn's room and saw the Erlenmeyer Flask in the daylight for the first time. She was a woman, with a long skirt, flared out at the bottom, pointing a pistol at SueAnn. Joe threw his beaker of water at her face, and she dropped the pistol. Joe had thrown the entire beaker at her; maybe he threw a bit harder than he intended, because the beaker broke when it hit her cheekbone, and caused blood to flow. Joe didn't notice the beaker problem until later because he followed the throw by rushing the lady and grabbing her pistol arm, even though it no longer held a pistol. One of SueAnn's students volunteered to get Mr. Hinkle, but because Hinkle had told Joe he'd be fired if one more attack occurred, he yelled, "No, don't go."

Then he added two words, more quietly, "Please don't."

The student returned to her seat, but Joe still had the 'Flask' by her arm and couldn't think what to do with her. SueAnn saw his indecision and suggested he tie her in the garage and call the Texas Rangers. Joe rushed out, tied the 'Flask' in his garage, and rushed back, in time for his class to start. He didn't, however, call the Rangers, but asked Sue to do that after they got home that evening. Junior called the school office before Joe and SueAnn were home and told June Arlington about the lady tied in their garage, so Mr. Hinkle found out, after all. And he tolerated it! The 'Flask' turned out to be the last attacker they had, so Joe and SueAnn were able to turn their full attention to their classes.